LOVE, LUST & LIES

Removing The Veil

Niesha M. Taylor

TABLE OF CONTENTS

ACKNOWLEDGMENTS

In the words of my beautiful late grandmother, Henry Ann Mayhorn, *Lord, I thank you!* God has been good to me and I thank him for keeping me when I thought I was about to lose my mind! Without him, I am nothing and all praises are due to him. Writing a book is harder than I thought and more rewarding than I could have ever imagined.

To the love of my life, my husband, Gregory V. Ray, Sr.. Thank you, baby, for loving me for me and for supporting all my dreams and aspirations. For 14 years, you have been more than a friend to me and now you are MY MVH (Most Valuable Husband). I love and appreciate you!

To my babies. Khallid, Daijah, A'niya, King David, and Laiya – Mommy loves you all so much and thank you for being great kids! It is because of you guys that I go so hard in all that I do. I sit back and watch you collectively and individually and all I can do is smile. The way all of you make sure I'm okay and the strength that is displayed from each of you is amazing, and it gives me the encouragement to keep going. Daddy would be so proud of you all just as am I. This is for the 5 of you!

To my family. My parents, Mack Taylor and Nyrah Taylor. I love you and thank you for the mating experience that created me. I would not be the woman I am today if it were not for the two of you. My siblings. Markees, thank you for always keeping it real. E, my baby! Thank you for the encouragement to never give up and for having my back. Marcus and Jessica, both of you stay working me, but I would not have it any other way. I love all of you and pray nothing but the best for all 5 of us. Auntie Sharon, I love you so much! Thank you for being that voice of reason, for always speaking the truth no matter what, and for being a second mother to me.

To my sister squad. Racheal, Shawntel, Airika, Temetres, Candice N., Candice C., Omesha, Kyran, Kirrtrina, Melissa, and Christine. You ladies mean the world to me. You all have seen me at my worst and were there to pull me right on up. Thank you for holding me accountable, for your encouragement, and for also being a listening ear when I needed it the most. You all are an inspiration to me, and I love you.

To my team, Adrienne E. Bell, Jeremiah Roberts, and Mel Shipman, thank you! None of this would be if it were not for you all. You all are amazing and have mastered every idea I had, and I'm blessed to have you all with me for the long haul.

My Guardian Angels. My grannies, Henry Ann Mayhorn and Retha Mae Smith, and my best friend, David Pickens, Jr.. There isn't a day or night that goes by that each of you aren't thought of and are greatly missed. Continue to rest in heaven while watching over the kids and I. We love each of you.

To my supporters. Thank you, thank you, thank you from the bottom of my heart for your love, support, inspiring texts, positive DM's, and prayers. The following from you all means the world to me and gives me yet another reason to continue doing what I'm doing. You all are awesome and I thank God for you all.

DEDICATION

This book is dedicated to all the men and women who are battling within themselves. It is never okay to settle to save face. Follow your heart and be free from the things that are holding you hostage.

INTRODUCTION
"LOVE OVERLOAD"

Have you ever loved someone so bad, but deep down knew THAT level of "love" could be toxic? Or, maybe you loved someone so much that the thought of them makes your heart skip a beat and you knew you couldn't live without them? Have you ever loved someone and wasn't afraid to shout it out to the mountains? Or have you ever loved someone so much, but you *had* to keep it bottled up in secrecy, tucked away to keep from being ridiculed?

Love has a powerful effect that should never be taken lightly. "I love you!" should have a genuine and passionate meaning behind it and should not be said to play on one's feelings. Love will have you acting in such a way that is unbelievable and doing things that is, in your mind, unexplainable.

"I have made some mistakes in my life but loving him was not one of them." – unknown

CHAPTER 1

CUPID'S ROMANCE

One Sunday morning, while the spirit was high and praise and worship was coming to an end, Marilyn spotted a young, handsome, caramelized complexion, 6'2 standing, Kobe Bryant look-alike walking in behind Pastor Randall with his chest out and head held high like he was the pastor. After assisting Pastor Randall to his seat, he struts to his seat while locking eyes with Marilyn, giving her the left eye Tupac wink and grin all in one motion. "My, my, my that is one good looking man right there. But why is this my first time seeing him?" Marilyn thought to herself. She quickly snapped out of it in time to sing with the Praise and Worship team after the announcements were done.

The church secretary approaches the podium. "Good morning, AOL Family! It is the 2nd Sunday of the month and it is also Youth Sunday. Today's announcements are: Immediately following service, ODM Dance Ministry will have a meeting. Please meet in the fellowship hall. Also, immediately after service, Pastor Lamont would like to meet with the youth board members. Please see Sis. Marilyn (Marilyn raises her hand) for an envelope for your dues. Lastly, Pastor Randall has a preaching engagement next Sunday at 3 pm at New Light C.O.G.I.C. All members are encouraged to travel with Pastor Randall to show support as our leader blesses others.

Are there any first-time visitors here with us?" About eight people stand and the congregation claps. "Amen. Here at Abundance of Life, we welcome you to join in with us by enjoying the presence of the Lord. We love you and pray that once you leave, you would return for more. Let us all stand to greet and love on our brothers and sisters in Christ. Amen."

During the visitors meet and greet, Marilyn noticed this man was approaching her. She begins to go the opposite way to greet the visitors when she realizes they are now face to face. "Hello Tootie!" he whispered in a sexy, deep, New Orleans accent as he leaned in for a church hug. "I saw you watching me and I must say that I've been watching you as well."

In a state of shock and denial, she gently backed away from him to keep from causing a scene and responded, "You don't know me like that to be calling my nickname." That wouldn't be the first time he'd call her that. Now with her back to him, she was grinning from ear to ear. After service ended, the meeting for O.D.M. began in the fellowship hall.

Walking in from the meeting with Youth Pastor Lamont, Marilyn is greeted by the director, who is also her mom, Sis. Smith. "Hey, baby! I would like to introduce you to Bro. Vernon Ray, Pastor's nephew. I've asked him and Pastor Lamont if they wouldn't mind helping us with the Easter skit. Bro. Vernon will be playing the role of one of the soldiers that helped crucify Jesus, played by Pastor Lamont."

Marilyn's look said something different, but "Oh, okay! That's great!" came out. As she tries to walk off, Sis. Smith grabs Marilyn by the hand.

"Um, that was rude! Aren't you going to speak?"

Marilyn is embarrassed, but while blushing she greeted the young man. "Hello Bro. Vernon! I'm Marilyn. Thank you for assisting O.D.M with our Easter skit. See you at rehearsal Thursday!"

"No problem! I'm here to help as much as I can," he responds while placing his hand on her left shoulder.

The past three days included non stop thinking about Pastor Randall's nephew, Vernon. Marilyn found herself daydreaming about him and was low-key excited to see him again since she missed bible study the night before. It is now 7 pm and the praise dance rehearsal has started.

"Okay, everyone! Let us bring our minds together and pray before we begin rehearsal. Everyone, bow your heads." Sis. Smith begins to pray.

"Wait a minute. Sorry, I'm late. I got off work later than expected. You mind if I pray?" Vernon managed to catch his breath from running into the fellowship hall. Marilyn never raised her head to see him come in, but her heart was beating at full speed just hearing him pray. "Heavenly father, in Jesus name, thank you for allowing us to wake up this morning with another opportunity to serve you. Thank you for keeping a hedge of protection around us and for granting us traveling grace to make it to your building. Lord, I ask that your spirit rest in this rehearsal tonight as we prepare to minister to your people about your son's death and resurrection. Let this dance minister to a lost soul, a broken heart, a suicidal thought, and even those in their right mind. God, I thank you for everyone here tonight and pray that our church continues to grow in love. I pray that we continue to grow in you. I ask these things according to your word. In Jesus name. Amen."

Once the prayer is done, Marilyn raises her head to see Vernon staring her down. She blushes again.

Sis. Smith exclaims, "Well thank you, Vernon, for that prayer. Ok, everyone! Places."

The music starts, people are crying, soldiers are yelling, and Jesus is being whipped. "It, it is finished! (pause) Why do you cry? He has risen. Why are you weeping? He's not deeeaaad...". Marilyn can feel Vernon's eyes watching her gracefully nail every move to the lyrics from afar in the sound booth.

"Man, she's so beautiful!" he thinks out loud.

"Bro! Is this why you decided to be here for your birthday instead of going out?" says Pastor Lamont.

"Nah dawg! I'm here to help with the Easter skit, but that Marilyn is beautiful," says Vernon.

"Well, why don't you shoot your shot?" asks Pastor Lamont. "She's my assistant for the youth department. She's a good girl and has her head on straight. She has one child, a son, but you can tell he's being raised to be a gentleman. Lil' Caleb! I'm going to see if she's dating anyone and let you know."

"Good looking out, lil bro, but I know she's not with anyone. I've been peeping her since before I moved down here via the videos on the church page. I'm not trippin' about her son. That's a plus! Another reason I'm attracted to her." says Vernon.

"There you go! Don't be trying to get with my assistant unless you're serious. She's tough and does not play!" says Pastor Lamar.

"Look, I got this. I got her and lil Caleb too!" assured Vernon.

Before Pastor Lamont could say something else, "Boy! What did you say about my nephew and my sister?! I'm going to tell her exactly what you said!" says Marilyn's sister, Nicole, as she's ear hustling on her way back into practice from the ladies' room.

"No need to. I can get her on my own. Matter of fact (Vernon rubs his hands together, winks his left eye, pulls out a cd from his back pocket that he made for her and holds it up), I already have her!" They all burst out laughing.

Nicole says sarcastically, "Awww!! Look at you. Showing your love for my sister through music. Y'all are too cute!"

Practice is now over and Vernon stops Marilyn before she walks outside. "Hey, Tootie!" Marilyn turns to him and gives him a look.

"Vernon, didn't I tell you before that you don't know me well enough to be calling me that?"

Marilyn doesn't notice that he's grinning from ear to ear at her feistiness. "Yeah, I know but looka, I wanted to give you this (he hands her the cd). Listen to it."

Marilyn looks at the cd written "Ray Love Mix CD" and her eyes widen. "Vernon, what is this?"

"Marilyn just listen to it!" he exclaims.

Marilyn gave him a look again. "Ok, if you insist."

* * *

"You don't have to turn the page, I read the story, it ends with you and me…" Marilyn is jamming to the cd Vernon gave her.

"Marilyn! Marilyn! Ma-ri-lynnnn!!!" Nicole comes running and yells into their room.

"What girl?! Why are you screaming my name like that as if somebody has died?" says Marilyn while turning the music down.

"Girl, guess what?!" Marilyn stands there with her arms folded. "Guess who's feeling you at church and swears up and down that he already got you AND Caleb?" Marilyn stands there, arms still folded, unbothered, with a nonchalant attitude. "Um, why you so tight? Chill a little!" Nicole says sarcastically. "Well, since you're dying to know, it's Vernon!" Marilyn begins to loosen a bit and show interest in the conversation Nicole is blabbing about, but tries her hardest to NOT let Nicole see her blushing.

"Toot, this nigga is feeling you hard! I overheard him and Pastor Lamont talking about you. Pastor was telling him about you and told him not to play if he's serious about getting at you. This fool Vernon then said he's been peeping you and Caleb, and he won't have a problem pulling you. Matter of fact, he claims he has you already!"

Marilyn is smiling big as day inside but has a 'whatever nigga' look on her face. "Well, what did you say when you overheard them talking?"

Nicole gives Marilyn the "now, you know what I did look". "Huh? Come on, Toot. YOU KNOW what I did. I popped in that convo like I was Peter Rabbit Jack in the box. Ears on alert!"

Marilyn begins to laugh, "Girl, you're retarded!"

"No seriously I did! I jumped all in their convo and asked Vernon what he said? And he repeated it word for word. No hesitation. Boo, he got it out for you and my baby Caleb. Did you hear me? I said you ANNND MY BABY, CALEB! This dude said Caleb gone be HIS lil junior. I told him that I was going to tell you too."

"And what did he say?" Marilyn asks curiously while turning to grab her tea.

"He said, "No need to! I can get her on my own. Matter of fact, I already have her!" Nicole tries to mimic Vernon's accent. "Oh, and he had this cd he pulled out saying it was for you. I laughed and told him, 'Awww!! Look at you. Showing your loooove for my sister through music. Yall are too cute!'. You know me, always with that sarcasm ish!"

Marilyn cannot hide the blush anymore. Nicole catches it this time. "And what exactly does that look mean, ma'am?!"

Marilyn blushes even harder. "Huh?! Nothing, gal! I have no clue what you're talking about."

Nicole now has that "DaeDae from 'Friday after Next' you-know-you-lying" look. "Bih, please! You know we *do not* keep secrets. Spill it!"

Marilyn spits out her tea from laughing at Nicole. "Girl, it's nothing!" as she wipes her mouth.

"Uh-huh! I saw you low-key blushing while I was telling you what was being said. That ninja got you whipped and he ain't even hit yet! Wait! Has he hit it? Oooh, I'm telling Moms you let the ninja smash and he JUST GOT TO THE CHURCH!"

Marilyn has a confused look and tries to respond but Nicole continues talking. "Toot! Really?! You know we were raised better than…"

Marilyn jumps in. "Girrrl! Pump yah breaks! Ain't nobody "smashed" nothing! I first saw him at church Sunday, and he was looking all spicy and things. He noticed that I was peeping him and of course I tried to play it off. During the meet and greet, he gave me that church hug to play it off, but whispered in my ear, 'Hello Tootie!'" Nicole is sitting with her mouth damn near to the floor. "That shocked the life out of my soul because he doesn't know me well enough to be calling me Tootie, and I think he knew it. But I didn't let him see that it did something to me. And are you talking about THIS cd?" Marilyn pulls it out of their cd player while blushing even harder.

Nicole then gives Marilyn that "yeah, he got you whipped" look on her face. "So, you mean to tell me this dude whispered all in your ear, hadn't hit, and now he thinks he has you with a cd? That boy is a fool!"

"Girl, hush! That's not all. He has a New Orleans accent and YOU KNOW I'm crazy about them N.O. boys. Anywho, so I'm guessing he found out that I also dance because Mama introduced him to me saying he's going to help us with the dance. In my head, I was saying, 'Good! I get to see him more,' but I played it off and said, 'That's great!' and walked off."

The two sisters both begin to laugh. "Why did your mammy grab me by the hand, pulled me back and said, 'That was rude!'? When I tell you that "embarrassed" is an understatement. I almost peeped myself!" said Marilyn. They laughed again! "Anywho, we talked for 10 more seconds and I thanked him for helping us. That was it! Now, while we were rehearsing, I noticed him watching me, but ignored it AND him," Marilyn said with a smile. "After all, I'm not really focused on dating."

"Bullshiiii!" Nicole says while fake sneezing. "Love birds at first sight... ahhh. Y'all ain't slick!"

* * *

It's Friday and Vernon is knocked out asleep in his bed.

"Son. Get up!" Pastor Randall says as he opens the curtains to let the sun in. "We have things to do! All this sleeping late isn't going to make your day a productive one."

With the pillow now over his face, Vernon mumbles, "Unc, I need about 20 more minutes to an hour!"

"For what? Been up thinking about that girl?" Vernon removes the pillow from his face. "Um-hum! You don't have to tell me. I already know! I'm far from crazy."

Vernon, with a slick grin, slyly asks, "What you mean, Unc?"

"Son, you know EXACTLY what and who I mean. You are MY nephew. It's no way possible YOU would join O.D.M just because. There's a motive behind this. Which one is it?"

"Come on, Unc! It ain't even like that. I'm there to help out."

Pastor Randall gives the side-eye. "Come on, Bruh! You can't pull one over on me, no! I know exactly which one it is too, but I'll sit back and watch what I'm thinking come to light. Now get up and get yourself ready so we can hit these streets. We have some things to do for this party you want."

"Alright, alright! I'm up! Good morning, Auntie!" Vernon calls to First Lady Kelly.

"Good morning, nephew! Long night? You're normally up before us, eating cereal and watching cartoons with the kids."

Vernon looks at Pastor Randall, who has the newspaper up to his face. "What do you mean, Auntie? I just wanted to get more rest before I hit the streets with Unc!"

"Yeah right! Sit down and eat your breakfast." Knowing an interrogation is about to take place, Vernon hesitates to sit. "So, son! Your uncle and I know the REAL reason you decided to join O.D.M and we know who she is. While we admire Sis. Smith's oldest daughter, Marilyn, we need you to focus on the situation you're facing. Now nephew, if you decide that you want to pursue Marilyn, keep it real with her and allow her to make her own decision if she wants to accept all that comes with that. Okay, son?"

With a grin on his face, "Yes, Auntie! I hear you loud and clear."

"Okay, Neph! Since you caught your aunt's drift, finish up with your food so we can roll out. I have a few other things to talk to you about," says Pastor Randall.

Vernon devours his food and heads out the door. "Alright, Auntie! I love you and see you later!"

"Alright baby, I love you too."

* * *

Pastor Randall and Vernon are in the truck headed to go shopping. "Alright, Vern! What is it about Marilyn that you love?" asked Pastor Randall.

"Wait! What? Love? Hold on, Bruh! I didn't say anything about loving her."

"My point exactly! You haven't said ANYTHING about her to your auntie and I. Normally, you come telling us about the first piece of you-know-what you come across and the outcome is never worth it. With Marilyn, you kept quiet! You sit and watch her every move at church, volunteering to help O.D.M out when you've never been interested in dance. I've caught you daydreaming about her and to top it off, Sis. Smith has come to your auntie and I saying you've approached her about dating her daughter. She gave you the okay because you were the first young man to approach her about her daughter."

Vernon has this twisted "did she really do that" look on his face. "Yes, bruh! She did really come to us. I honestly do not want you to pursue her because of your situation. She has a son and…"

"What about her son?" Vernon cuts Pastor Randall off mid-sentence. "I'm not blind to the fact that she has a son, no! He's one of the reasons I'm digging her. Lil' Caleb gone be my lil' man, yah heard me! And since you asked, yes, I am digging her, and it very well may be that I love her too. Most times when I'm thinking about her, I begin to smile at my thoughts of her. Bruh! Me, Ray Love? Smiling? Behind a female? It gotta be something like love and I'm bound to find out. Matter of fact, I'ma get at her at this dinner tonight!"

"Bruh, what?" replies Pastor Randall.

"Unc, I'ma invite her to come."

"Pump ya brakes! You may want to check with your boy Lamont to make sure he doesn't have her booked to do something for hi…."

Vernon interrupts again. "Yeah, about that! I already checked that when he was explaining who she is and what she does around the church. He TRIED to put ME in the door (Vernon does air quotations with his hands) with her, but I told him I didn't need his assistance to get his assistant."

"Okay, pimp! I see you got this all figured out," Pastor R responds sarcastically. "Again, remember what your auntie told you. Tell Marilyn what's going on with you. She deserves the ability to choose to be with you or not."

"Unc! Bruh! I got this! Now, let's get this fit for my day, brother!"

* * *

After a few hours of shopping and handling business, Pastor Randall stops by the church for a meeting with the Men's Ministry. Vernon notices the Music Ministry is also there having rehearsal. As he makes his way to one of the meeting rooms, he notices that Marilyn is not on stage rehearsing. "Where is she?" he mumbled to himself.

"Lord, you are good. You've been so good. Lord, you are good. You've been better than good." Vernon hears her voice coming from the direction of the ladies' room. "I can't thank you enough. I owe you my liiii." Marilyn stops singing when she sees Vernon and tries to walk right past him. "Hey, Vernon! How are you doing? Been rehearsing your part for the resurrection skit?" She pats him on the shoulder while continuing to walk.

He grabs her hand to stop her. "Hey, Marilyn! Hold on a sec." Marilyn's heart begins to beat fast. "Yes, I've been rehearsing and I've got my lines almost memorized. But look, I'm having a small dinner at this restaurant called Grand Lux in the Galleria at 8 pm. I'm person-ally inviting you, your mom, and sister to come. Are you guys free?!"

Vernon is lowkey nervous, but won't dare let Marilyn see that... at least not yet. "Oh, Vernon! It was nice of you to invite us. I think my mom has plans tonight, but I'll see if I can get my son's father to babysit so my sister and I can stop by. No promises though!" Marilyn says with a slight blush. "Okay Vernon, I gotta get back to rehearsal."

"Ok, my love! Talk to you soon!" he responds. "She's going to come. At least I hope so," he whispers to himself as he walks into the meeting.

* * *

It is 8:05 pm and Marilyn hasn't made it yet. "Where is she?" Vernon mumbles while trying to entertain everyone that is there waiting to be seated.

"Hey, Vern!" a group of women surrounds him while he's at the door awaiting Marilyn's arrival.

"What's good?! I wasn't expecting to run into y'all," responds Vernon with a shocked look on his face.

"Yeah, we know! Kia couldn't make it, so she asked us to come in her absence." Kia's cousin, Tamika replies.

"Kia? Who told her I would be here? Man, I gotta get these girls from around me before Marilyn gets here. They gone mess everything up." Vernon says to himself. "Oh ok! Well, it was good to see y'all! Do enjoy yourselves!" he says to the women.

"Um, Vern! We came to turn up with you and your people. What's up? You expecting someone in place of Kia to show up?"

Vernon responds, "Shay, what are you talking about? Y'all my people too. Besides, Kia and I are no longer..." He stops mid-sentence when he spots Marilyn walking in with her sisters, Nicole and Cara. Tamika notices his facial expression and demeanor change as Marilyn walks in. She calls Kia right away as Vernon dismisses himself from them to greet Marilyn. "Aight yall, I gotta go!"

"Hey my love, Ms. Marilyn! I'm glad you and your sisters could make it. Hello, Nicole and Cara! Thank you both for coming through."

"No problem, Vernon! Thank you for inviting us. You two love birds go talk or something. We're going to the bar!" Nicole replies while Cara laughs. They walk off.

Embarrassed by her sisters, Marilyn blushes and hugs Vernon. "Hey, Vernon! Thank you again for inviting us. This is a nice place."

"No! Thank you for coming! You look so beautiful tonight, just as you do every time I see you."

"Thank you, sir! I just threw this together. You're looking handsome tonight. All fresh. I see you! You must have a date after this!" Marilyn says, trying to throw him off.

"Yep! I sure do. YOU!" Vernon's response threw Marilyn off.

Standing there stunned at the certainty that Vernon displays, Marilyn quickly gathers her thoughts and facial expressions. "Alrighty then! So about how much longer before we can all sit to eat?" Marilyn tries to change the subject.

"In a few but until then, what's up with you? By now, I think you know that I'm interested in Ms. Tootie (Marilyn gives him the side-eye), yeah. So, what's up?" Vernon says to Marilyn in a tone soothing to her soul.

"Well um, I am sing…"

Marilyn is interrupted by the hostess. "Party of 20 for Randall. Party of 20 for Randall!" she says.

"Well, I guess we better get seated. You can sit by me. We'll finish our conversation later," Vernon insists. He grabs Marilyn by the hand as they walk to their seat. Marilyn is flattered that this man who doesn't know anything about her has taken such interest in her. She couldn't begin to understand why especially since she had joined the church only five months prior.

Everyone is seated and Vernon stands up to thank everyone for coming while the waitress starts taking drink orders.

"Toot!" Nicole mumbles under her breath while Vernon is talking.

"What, guhl?" Marilyn whispers back. "Girl, I saw him grab your hand to walk with him to the table. What? Y'all a couple now? Don't worry. Tell me the details later but um, I need you to keep your eyes open and watch these unfamiliar faces."

Marilyn looks around as if she is looking for the waitress to take her drink order and spots two females eyeing her down.

"Yeah, those 2! I overheard them telling somebody named Kia about Vernon and how he was talking to 'some girl'. I almost said something. You know me. I don't give a flying flip, but because we're out with Pastor and a few of the members from church, I let they ass make it," says Nicole.

"I'm not worried about them. AT ALL! He and I aren't even friends yet. Just church members." Marilyn implies.

"Toot! Please. You know that fool into you MORE than being 'church members.' Hell, more than just future 'friends.' Anyway, just peep the scene." Nicole warns.

"Alright, crazy girl!" says Marilyn.

"Excuse me, ladies! What would you like to drink? And are you ready to place your order?" asks the waitress.

"Yes, please! I'll take ice water with fresh lemons and cherries on the side. For my food, I will have the Chicken Royale with asparagus added on the side. Please," orders Marilyn. Nicole and Cara ordered their dinner next.

Shortly after the food was served, laughter rang among the table and monetary gifts were given. "So Tootie!" Vernon says to get Marilyn's attention.

"You mean, Marilyn!" she snaps back with a slight grin.

He laughs. "Ok, Miss Marilyn! What's up? You okay? Enjoying yourself?"

"Yes, yes, and yes." Marilyn repeats. As everyone was preparing to pay and leave, Marilyn signaled to Vernon that she and her sisters were leaving. "Good night everyone! You all have a safe drive home." says Marilyn to her church family.

"Hold on, let me walk you and your sisters out." Vernon insists. They all walk outside. Nicole and Cara get inside the truck. "Thank you, again, Vernon, for inviting me and my sisters to your dinner party," says Marilyn.

"The pleasure was mine! Listen, from our little conversation earlier, I know you are single. I did my research." Vernon says with a smile on his face. "I would like to take you out on an official date if you don't mind. Here is my number." Vernon hands Marilyn his number. "Call me so I can get to know you more." Vernon then opens the door for Marilyn to get in.

"Oh, wait! I forgot to grab your gift out the trunk before coming in and almost forgot it again." Marilyn says while walking back to the trunk. As she opens the trunk to grab Vernon's gift and turns around to give it to him, he grabs her gently by the face and kisses her passionately. Thinking she would cut it short; Marilyn engages. "Man, get a room! We do not want to see that!" blurts out Nicole.

Laughing to themselves, Vernon says, "Goodnight, Ms. Marilyn! I look forward to hearing from you soon! Thank you for the gift.

Y'all be careful going home, now!" With a smile on her face, blushing, Marilyn replies, "You too, Vernon! Good night."

* * *

The ride is silent on the way home. Cara is in the back seat with earphones on, Nicole is on her phone, and Marilyn is in a daze after what just happened between her and Vernon. "Snap out of it!" says Nicole while snapping Marilyn back into reality. "It was just a kiss! You can't be THAT sprung already."

"Shut up guhl!" Marilyn snaps back. "Although it was JUST a kiss, it was the passion behind it. He meant that kiss!" Marilyn says while blushing through her smile. *As soon as I get home, I am going to call him. Nah, I better not. I don't want him thinking he got it like that just yet."*

"Chile please, he does have it like that, and you KNOW you gon call him as SOON as you get home."

"Nicole, you talk too much and don't know what the heck you are talking about!"

Marilyn, Nicole, and Cara all look at each other for a second, then burst out laughing. "Now, Toot! You know dang on well I KNOW WHAT I'M TALKING ABOUT!" Nicole says while laughing. "I'm the one that told you what I overheard and everything I told you he said, he told you himself."

Marilyn laughs and rolls her eyes at the same time. "I guess you do know, huh?!" They arrive home. Marilyn throws the car in park and runs upstairs to their apartment to call Vernon. Before grabbing the phone, Marilyn hesitates for a brief second. *Should I call right now? Maybe he has not made it home yet. Nah, do not call right now. Call in an hour.* Marilyn waits before calling him and continues thinking about that kiss.

CHAPTER 2

PERFECT LOVER,
PERFECT FRIEND

The next morning, the phone rings.

"Well good morning, Ms. Marilyn! I've been waiting on your call," says Vernon in the most soothing morning voice one could ever hear.

"Well, how are you this morning, Vernon? Long night?" says Marilyn.

"Not at all! Left after you did...well, after telling all my guests good night. I was hoping you would call while on the way home. I figured you didn't due to your sisters being in the car. Overall, I'm better now that you're on the phone. So, what's up? When can I take you out?"

Marilyn pauses. "Now Vernon, let us not sit here and act as if last night didn't take place." Marilyn thought about that moment she and Vernon shared at the trunk of her truck all night.

"About that!" says Vernon. "I'm sure you didn't expect that, but that's how I felt at that moment. It's how I feel right now. So, you gon let me take you out?" Vernon asks in a tantalizing manner. "If you're available; we can hang out today."

"Ok, Vernon! I'm okay with that. What do you have in mind? Where should I meet you and what time?" responds Marilyn.

"The Butterfly Center. 11 am!" Vernon immediately responds as if he had this preplanned. "Then, brunch afterwards?"

"Well look at you! I sense you already had this in your head and was waiting on the right time to ask me out. Would this be the one at the museum by Hermann Park?" Marilyn asks while stunned, grinning hard, thanking God in her head that Vernon cannot see her.

"Yes, and you're absolutely right Marilyn. Since I have been here, I've always wanted to go but only wanted the right one to take with me."

Marilyn's eyes widen and she's still grinning from ear to ear. What Vernon does not know is that Marilyn loves butterflies. Or *does* he know? "That is sweet of you, Vernon! Of course, I'd love to come with you. See you in a bit."

About 3 hours later, Vernon and Marilyn find a nearby place to eat. As they are ordering their food, Vernon says, "Hey, Marilyn! There's something I need to tell you and I hope it doesn't run you away!"

Marilyn looks at Vernon, squinting, and says "I'm listening..."

Vernon does not hesitate to open up, "Well, I'm in trouble with the law and may be going away for some time." Before Marilyn could ask what happened, Vernon went straight into it. "My son was crying uncontrollably, and I was trying to calm him down by doing anything I thought would help." Vernon's eyes began to water as he was speaking. "I was tossing him up and down on the bed, and he fell off! I hurried to pick him up, console him, and he eventually stopped crying. I laid him down next to me and we both went to sleep. Next thing, I wake up and he's shaking. I attempted to do CPR. I called his mom, the police, and my uncle. I take full responsibility for my son's passing and live with this regret and pain. I know you have Caleb and understand if you choose to not deal with me. I under..."

Marilyn cuts Vernon off with a smile and responds in a firm, but soothing voice, "Vernon! Calm down and take a breather! It's okay! You will be okay. I'm sorry for your loss and I'm right here!" At that very moment, Vernon knew he loved her for sure and although he wanted her to himself, he knew it wouldn't be fair to her if he received a long sentence.

✳ ✳ ✳

While in the car on the way home, Vernon wasn't his normal, conversation-starting self. He was quiet and had a look of wonder on his face. Marilyn reaches over and grabs his hand, "Vernon! What's on your mind? You're quiet and that's not normal for you."

Vernon looks at her and asks, "Are you sure you're okay with what I shared with you? I was hoping you said what you said, but it was still a shock for me."

Marilyn gives Vernon a reassured gesture by grabbing his hand tighter and responding, "Yes, I'm sure!"

They arrive back at Marilyn's home and Vernon walks her to the door. "Marilyn, thank you for not judging me. I really appreciate that!"

"Vernon, we all make mistakes and I, for one, have no room to judge anyone. I meant what I said. I'm here for you!" She reaches up to give him a kiss. "Good night, Vernon! Call me when you make it home."

From that moment on for about a year, Vernon and Marilyn would spend plenty of time together, learning each other. That included breakfast before church, going out to eat after church was over and walks/picnics at the park. At that point, Marilyn introduces Caleb to Vernon.

"What's up Lil' Caleb! How are you, man? I'm Vernon!" Vernon reaches out to dab Caleb.

Waving back instead, "Hey!" Caleb responds.

Vernon kneels to get to Caleb's level. "How old are you? Do you like sports?"

"I'm 3. I like Spiderman!" Caleb responds in the most innocent 3-year-old voice.

"That's cool, lil' man. I will have to get you something Spiderman then. Will you like that?" Caleb looks at Marilyn for reassurance. Marilyn smiles. Caleb looks back at Vernon and nods his head yes. They became buddies from that moment on.

At this point, it was understood that Vernon and Marilyn were "together" and were always doing something with Caleb right there with them. Vernon said this is what he wanted and was going to get. And he was right.

* * *

It wasn't until Friday night when Vernon asked Marilyn on another date; this time, back at Grand Lux and he told her to be ready at 7. Vernon knocks on the door of Ms. Smith. "Well hello, Vernon! I'm assuming you're here for Marilyn since there's no practice tonight. Come on in, son! She'll be out in a sec. She's putting Caleb to sleep," says Ms. Smith as she sits back in her chair to watch her shows. "So! Where y'all going this time?! Wherever it is, just make sure you **A.** treat her with respect and **B.** have her back at a decent time."

Marilyn walks in blushing. "Mama, what are you in here talking about?! Hey, Vernon!"

Vernon can see her blushing. "Hello, beautiful!" Vernon says with a look of desire in his eyes. Are you ready to ride?"

"Yes. I am,l now that Caleb is asleep. Bye, mama! I'll be back soon." says Marilyn.

"Have fun y'all! Call me if you need me," says Ms. Smith.

Riding in the car listening to India Arie's "The Truth", Vernon turns the radio down. "So, Ms. Marilyn! Why are you so quiet?" he asks while reaching over to grab her hand.

"No reason in particular. Just thinking about some things!" she responds. They pull up to Grand Lux and go inside to be seated.

While standing there waiting, Vernon asks "You wanna place a to-go order and we go somewhere much quieter to talk?"

"That's perfectly fine with me!" responds Marilyn. They order their food to go and a short time later, they leave Grand Lux with their dinner.

* * *

"So beautiful, I have somewhere we can go to chill, relax and talk."

"Ok cool. Where to?!" Marilyn responds as she realizes they are pulling up to the Westin Galleria.

Sitting in valet, Vernon gets out to open the door for Marilyn and grabs the food. As they walk towards the elevator, Marilyn says, "So, you're telling me you had this night pre-planned because you certainly didn't stop to check in/grab a room key."

Vernon smiles as they enter the elevator. "You guessed it!"

She looks him upside his head and smiles. "I know." He responds again in a confident voice. Exiting the elevator on floor 20, they proceed to the room. Vernon opens the door; Marilyn's mouth drops as he signals for her to walk in before him. Purple tulips everywhere, candles lit with champagne on ice sitting on a table near the balcony.

Definitely an environment to relax, chill, and talk... Marilyn thinks to herself. "Now Vernon, this is beautiful! What's all this for?"

Vernon puts the food in the kitchen, grabs a remote and turns some music on low. "It's for you, my baby! This is what you deserve."

As they get comfortable to relax and eat, Vernon asks Marilyn about what was on her mind while in the car. "Well, nothing really! Just the fact that I'm really into you and love the way you treat my son." Marilyn tells Vernon. "I'm very particular with who I let around my son. After hearing and seeing how into us you are has done it for me."

"Well, that comes with wanting to be with you. I have to accept him. No other way around it. That's my lil' dude, Caleb!"

Marilyn blushes as she gets up to put the food away and walks over to the table to pour them some champagne. Vernon gets up and walks up behind her. Moving her hair to the left side of her neck, he leans in and kisses her on the right side. Marilyn freezes for a sec with her eyes closed and before submitting to her desires to have him and his to have her, she quickly turns around face to face with Vernon. Before she can speak, he softly grabs her by the neck and kisses her gently yet repeatedly. As the sexual desire of wanting each other rises between the two, Vernon sticks his hand under her shirt, unhooks her bra, slides her straps down, and slips it off.

He lifts her arms up to pull her shirt off. While they grind their hips together, Marilyn unbuckles Vernon's pants. They drop to the floor and she feels him throbbing for her attention. She slides her hands inside his boxers to calm him down, but it doesn't help. She then caresses his chest as he takes his shirt off. Now chest to chest, he makes his way from her mouth, to her neck again, and licks her slowly from her collarbone down to her left nipple. Vernon sucks softly while biting and licking softly. Over to the right breast, he does the same thing. He then makes his way down and while unbuckling her pants. He can smell that she's ready for him. He slides her pants down, kisses her inner thighs, shins, feet, and licks his way all the way back up to her pelvis while looking her in her eyes.

Continuing up, he licks her stomach, breasts, ears and back to her mouth, kissing her passionately. Breaking away from the kiss, he asks "Do you trust me?!"

"Yes, Vernon! I trust you." Marilyn responds. Vernon then begins to take her lace panties off. Standing there admiring her birthday suit, he finishes taking off his boxer briefs. Marilyn's eyes widen when she sees he's at full attention and smiles.

"You like what you see?" he asks.

"Yes indeed!"

He walks up to her and grabs her hand, walking towards the bed. He asks her one more time, "Tootie, do you trust me?!"

"Yes, I do!"

He then gestures Marilyn to sit on the edge of the bed. He walks up to her, penis in face, but guides her to slide back as he kisses her all over again.

As she is laying there, he makes his way to her honey pot and kisses her softly on her yoni. Letting out a soft moan, Marilyn widens her legs. Vernon takes his time with Marilyn, making sure he slurps every bit of her release. He looks up at her and says, "I'm putting my name all over this…" as he begins to devour her juices."

"V.E.R.N.O.N." Marilyn is moaning louder and louder as he pleases her to complete release.

As Vernon comes up for air, he smiles at her and asks, "You good, baby?"

"I will be even more once you give me what you've been wanting to give me!" as she sits up, gesturing to him to get in bed with her.

Climbing in bed with her, Marilyn grabs him feeling how hard he is. She guides him inside her, arching her back as he pushes all the way in her, nice and slow. Marilyn lets out a vulnerable moan. In and out, slowly, he penetrates her being, whispering her name "Marilyn" as she grips him. The desire they've been having for each other has taken its course. Full-fledged intimacy.

Vernon looks Marilyn in the eyes and says one more time, "Tell me you trust me!"

"I trust you, baby!" As Marilyn is responding, they both reach that release together while looking each other in the eyes.

Vernon kisses Marilyn softly and says, "I love you!"

Marilyn's heart begins to beat faster and faster. "I love you too!" while rubbing his face as he lays on top of her. That type of intimacy between Marilyn and Vernon would go on for about a year.

* * *

Months turned into days that are quickly approaching for Vernon to leave Marilyn. At least that's how she looked at it. Marilyn calls Vernon to come over so they can talk.

"Good morning, my baby! What's going on?" answers Vernon.

"Do you have to work today? If not, come over here. I need to see and talk to you," replied Marilyn.

"Of course, I do have to work but I'll come see you before I head in. Be there in an hour."

Vernon pulls up at Ms. Smith's house to chill with Marilyn. "Hey, baby!" Marilyn greets Vernon at the door with a kiss. He comes in, gets settled and they begin to eat the breakfast that Marilyn prepared.

"So, what's up my love? Where's Caleb and what you want to talk about?" Vernon says with a slightly full mouth.

"Caleb is with his dad for two weeks and I want to talk about us! When you leave, what will be the plan for us?"

"Well, I would love to have you on my side as you have been supportive of me."

"Well, that goes without saying, Vernon! I'm talking about us. Becoming official. While I know you don't want to put titles on us because you're not sure what the outcome will be, I need you to know that I'm here. I'm not going anywhere!"

"I know, my baby! I know you got me. I know you want us to be US. I want the same thing, but I feel it's best we wait at least until my court hearing when I find out the outcome."

"Okay, baby! I understand," Marilyn responds but inside, she's hurt. She's in love with Vernon, but doesn't want to pressure him. "Well, isn't it time for you to get going so you won't be late to work?"

Vernon has a grin on his face. "Not anymore." He responds as he gets up from the table headed to the living room. "When you call, work is no longer important. I called in so I can spend more time with you before my court hearing in case they try and give me some big time. This is my last week anyway." Vernon says. Marilyn now has this seductive grin on her face. She pushes him on to the living room couch and they get it in. Vernon is there pretty much all day until Ms. Smith calls to let Marilyn know she is on her way home.

"Hey, Mama! What's up?" "I'm on my way home, but I'm about to stop and get something to eat. You want something?"

"No ma'am! Vernon just got here and we're about to leave to go eat. Caleb is gone with BJ for two weeks, so I may be gone too."

"Ok, Marilyn! You know the rules. If you are not back by a certain time, my doors will be locked and I'm not getting up to unlock them. Stay where you are."

"Yes mama! I know. I love you. Talk to you later."

"Love you, too!"

Vernon and Marilyn leave to go eat and then get a room for the night. "Marilyn baby, we keep going like this, you gon end up pregnant," Vernon says.

"That's what you want anyway as much as you say that. I wouldn't mind giving you another child too," responds Marilyn. Neither of them knew that THAT would happen.

A month and a half later, Vernon's court hearing arrived. Vernon and Marilyn have one last "good time" before he must turn himself in. The next day, Marilyn had to babysit her godsister's baby and wasn't able to make it to the hearing. Vernon knew this and reassured Marilyn that he loved her and that everything would be okay especially since Ms. Smith would be there. After becoming sick, Marilyn decided to take a pregnancy test that gave a positive result. Excited and scared at the same time, Marilyn didn't have a clue how she would tell Vernon.

He's now gone after learning he was given 30 years from her mom. "Thirty years..." she thought to herself. Hearing "thirty years", not knowing about the prison system to begin looking for him, *AND* not being able to hear Vernon's calming voice to tell him the good news took over and eventually Marilyn miscarried.

That was the most devastating moment of her life. Vernon has been wanting another baby and wanted one with his love, Marilyn. "I will never tell him that we conceived. I don't want to stress him more than what he'll already be," says Marilyn to herself.

It would be 2008 before Marilyn heard Vernon's soothing New Orleans accent. As Marilyn and Caleb were sleeping, Marilyn's phone began to ring. Thinking it was Nicole, she answered.

"Hello, Beautiful! Do you still love me?" It was Vernon.

Marilyn woke the hell up and was geeked to talk to her baby! "Yes, I still love you and miss you so much! I just knew you would forget about me!" Marilyn responds.

"I love you too and why would I forget about you? You my baby and I have been thinking about you nonstop. How have you been? What is Caleb up to?" says Vernon.

"I've been okay! Just working and thinking about you. Caleb is great! Being a kid riding his lil' skateboard."

"Man, I miss yall, yeah! They gave me 30 years and I have been trying to reach out to you for the longest to tell you what happened. What's the address so I can write to you?"

After giving Vernon the address, Marilyn only had enough time left to tell him how much she loved him and vice versa before they had to get off the phone. Thank God she answered because that conversation was over just as quick as it started. That would be the only time she would talk to him. However, their relationship grew closer and closer once they started to write to each other. Still no "title", but they knew what it was. Although their bond was strong, Marilyn would often have the thought of Vernon forgetting about her over the course of the time he'd be in prison. If she decided to wait for him, her life would have passed her by. So, she figured it would be best for her to find a way to move on with her own life.

CHAPTER 3

SWEET DREAMS &
BEAUTIFUL NIGHTMARES

In February 2009, Marilyn began working for Walmart as the greeter. One day, while greeting all the customers entering or exiting, she noticed one customer that stood out by the way he walked, however, she paid him no mind. While continuing to do her job, she turned around to address a coworker of hers, who seemingly was interested in her, and noticed this same customer now standing inside McDonald's, eye-balling her. Not interested at all, Marilyn gave him the "What are you looking at?" glare thinking it would scare him off, but it didn't. In fact, Marilyn's mean look was the ammo to his G42 380. Completely ignoring that she was in mid-conversation with her co-worker, he made his way to her area and boldly introduced himself. Tapping her on her shoulder, "Hello, ma'am! How you doin'? My name's David. You gone talk to me like you were talking to him?"

David was sweet on the eyes and had a swag about him that made Marilyn blush, yet it was his confidence in knowing he was about to "tag you're it" her that made her oblige, but he wouldn't know it.

"Hello, David! That was rude of you, but how are you doing?" Marilyn said with a smile.

"I'm doing much better now that you're talking to me! So, what's up? You look real familiar. I met you in Coco Loco or was it Pink Panties?" David asks.

"Yeah, so you look familiar as well and you probably did see me in Coco Loco posted up because I sure as hell wasn't on the dance floor. You look like one of those dudes that was trying to holler and got mad cause I turned you down! Now, I know for damn sure you haven't seen me in no fish smelling Pink Panties! I've been there one time and ain't never went back. You outta line for even thinking that." Marilyn responded.

"Nah! If you did see me, it wasn't recent. I just came home from doing a lil time."

Marilyn gave David the side-eye. They both started laughing. "What did you do to get locked up?" Marilyn asked.

"Aggravated assault with a deadly weapon on a family member. Speaking of, I gotta get to this anger management class." David replied.

"Okay!" Marilyn responds as if that was a bit much. Realizing that the end of her shift was approaching and David realizing that he needed to get to his class, he gave her his number.

"Here's my number! If you call me, that'll let me know you're interested in me."

* * *

Three hours after making it home, Marilyn decides to call David.
"Hello," he whispers.
"Hey David, this Marilyn!"
"Oh, what's up? Say lookout. I'm in this class and as soon as I get out I'ma hit you back. Aight!"
"Oh my bad! I'm sorry! Yea call me later." Marilyn hangs up and waits for David to call back. About an hour later David calls her back.
"Hey Marilyn! This David. What's up? You couldn't wait to call a nigga, huh?"

"Boy please, don't flatter yourself. I was digging our convo earlier and decided to call you," says Marilyn.

"So, you got any plans tonight?" asks David.

"Not at all!! My son is gone, so I'm just chillin' tonight. You?"

"You have a son? I have a daughter and she's with her mom, so I'm free if you wanna hang!"

"Yeah that's cool with me. I'll send you the address to come pick me up."

"Bet," replies David.

Marilyn, for some reason, felt safe enough with David to be giving him her address. It could be that "Prison Life" turned her on and the swag of David made her want him sexually, right away. Prison would also be the reason he wanted her in that way as well. He arrives at her apartment to pick her up and they head to his place.

"So, Mr. David! What are we doing tonight?" Marilyn asks, playing dumb.

"If you want, we can go to my place, chill, and watch movies."

"Sounds like a plan to me!" responds Marilyn.

"Aight bet!"

* * *

About 10 minutes later, they arrived at the Monticello Apartments on Ella. David gets out and opens the door for Marilyn. They walk into the apartment and immediately Marilyn notices that another woman's touch is there. Not to mention the pictures of their little family on the wall.

"So, David...who is she if you don't mind me asking?"

"That's my EX Girlfriend, Andrea. Ex because I found out she been messing with some nigga while I was gone. She gone outta town with that nigga now and when she get back all my shit will be back at my grandpa's house. Fuck her!" he responds.

"Okayyy!! Marilyn sits on the couch. "You have a beautiful little girl by the way!"

"Thank you! That's my baby, Angel! So anyway, what you wanna watch?" he asks while laying on the couch, on Marilyn's lap.

"Um, you a bit too comfortable, aren't you?!" Marilyn suggests.

"Oh, my bad, I figured since you're in my space that you didn't mind."

Marilyn looked into David's brown eyes and started to blush. "David you're fine! So, what's up? I wanna know what happened that led you to prison." she asks.

"Basically, I beat my mama's husband ass for putting his hands on her. That nigga called the police on me and I went to jail. Thinking she would leave his ass, she stayed her crazy ass with him. Damn near didn't graduate high school behind their ass. Shit pissed me off! I didn't talk to my mama for a whole year after that shit."

"Ok we can change the subject. I can see and tell that really bothers you. So, what movie are we about to watch?" asks Marilyn.

"Um, you pick while I go take a shower." David jumps up to go take a shower. Marilyn gets up to continue looking at the pictures on the wall. As she's walking around the living room, she hears the water running to the shower as if David purposely left the door open. She walks into the hallway and sees David's fine ass naked in the shower. Marilyn stands there admiring him. David sees her and asks, "You like what you see?"

"HELL YEAH!" Marilyn responds in her head, but says out loud, "You aight!" and starts laughing. "What I'm trying to figure out is why are you so comfortable taking a shower with the door open and you don't know me."

"Easy!" he replies. "When you're in prison with strangers, you adapt to your surroundings. I aint no dirty nigga so I'm taking me a shower and don't care who looking."

"That makes sense!" Marilyn responds.

David hops out the shower, grabs a towel to dry off while approaching Marilyn.

"And again, you're in my place and I know you enjoyed watching me!" he continues. Marilyn rolls her eyes but is blushing even harder. "So, what's up? We going in the bedroom or living room?" he asks.

"Your place, remember? You decide." Marilyn snaps back. He leads her to the bedroom, undresses her, and has her to lay down. "The only thing I want you to do is lay here and enjoy." David told Marilyn. He then kisses her from the neck down to her honey pot and stays there for a while. After bringing her to an orgasm, he grabs a condom to put on and slides into her. After a few strokes, he says, "Damn, girl! You feel good as hell!" Marilyn is too busy trying to hold her moan in that she doesn't respond to him verbally but does so by releasing herself yet again. They would continue all night.

* * *

Back at Marilyn's apartment, David walks her to the door and kisses her goodnight. "Aight, Marilyn! Have a great night! I'll call you when I make it back to the crib." David tells her.

"Okay, cool and thank you!" as she blushes. Not even twenty minutes later, the two get on the phone and talk all night. Eventually, Marilyn would quickly learn the type of man David was... especially behind his daughter, Angel.

* * *

After a week of getting to know one another by phone, David decides to introduce Marilyn to his daughter. He calls Marilyn to let her know he was on his way over to see her.

"Hey Marilyn! I'm picking my daughter up then we gone head over to see you. That's cool?"

Marilyn hears loud talking in the background. "Yes, David! That's cool. I can't wait to meet her as much as you talk about her."

"Bet!" David responds. About 15 minutes later, David pulls up to Marilyn's with his nephew and daughter. "Hey Marilyn!" He hugs her. "This is my nephew, D, and my baby girl, Angel!"

"Hey! How are you?" Marilyn says to David's nephew while turning her attention to his daughter. "Hey baby girl! I'm Marilyn. How old are you?" Marilyn asks Angel. She holds up 3 fingers and starts to smile. "She's too cute!" Marilyn tells David while reaching for Angel. "You gon let me hold you?" Marilyn says to Angel as she leans in for Marilyn to hold her. "Aww! She's too sweet!" Marilyn exclaims.

"Yeah man, this my baby girl. I love this little girl. Just can't stand her crazy ass mama. All that shit she was talking in the background while I was talking to you. She doesn't want Angel around you for some reason. We got into it the other day cause she saw your name in my phone. I told her to mind her fucking business especially when she went out of town with fat boy!"

Marilyn is now looking thrown off. "Umm! Why would she not want her daughter around me? I don't know her or you like that and haven't done anything. Hell, we just started talking! Y'all on that bullshit!"

David laughs. "Nah! That's her retarded ass! I don't give a damn what she talking about. I got my daughter and that's all that matters" His cell phone rings. "Damn! Here go her throwed off ass now! What's up, man? What you want? Bring her to you? For what? I just picked her up from you. We chillin' right now!" David puts her on speaker.

"David, bring my damn baby back to my job. I told yo ass I don't want her around no other bitches you fucking!" Whatever David said to Angel's mom after that, Marilyn didn't hear it. Her antennas went up when she heard "bitches you fucking" and wanted to fight her. "Marilyn, my bad!" David says. "Let me get my daughter to her stupid ass mama and I'll be back to see you in a few."

"Yeah, you do that cause she don't know me but best believe she can get these hands. You be careful going over there and don't be arguing with that girl and end up back in prison." Marilyn developed a soft spot for David quicker than normal and didn't want him to be taken back to prison behind his baby mama. "Call me when you get there AND DO NOT GET INTO IT WITH THAT GIRL!" Marilyn says to David.

"Trust me, I won't!" David reassured Marilyn.

* * *

About fifteen minutes later, Marilyn calls David to make sure they are okay.

"Hello! Hello!" David's nephew, D, answered the phone.

"Where is David?" Marilyn asks.

"He's arguing with this girl. She tried to take his keys to keep him here. He got them back but chucked her purse on top of the house. Now she is trying to hit him!"

Marilyn has heard enough. "Tell me how to get to y'all. I'm on my way," says Marilyn. D struggles with telling her exactly how to get there but eventually, she finds them. David sees her and attempts to get in his car to leave while his baby mama is still after him. He signals Marilyn to stay in her car. Andrea sees her.

"Oh, so you told this bitch where I work?" Andrea has a home healthcare job. "You really got me fucked up!" Andrea says to David but before she realizes it, Marilyn is out of the car after hearing "bitch" again.

"Who the fuck you calling a bitch, bitch! Come see about me then!" Marilyn says to Andrea. Before Marilyn can get all the way around her car, David's nephew grabs her and pulls her back to her car while David is yelling at Andrea to take her stupid ass back in the house. He, once again, signals Marilyn to *calm down and let's go*. They leave. Shortly after they leave, Marilyn looks in her rearview mirror and notices his baby mama behind her, seemingly wanting to run her off the road. That took the cake. Marilyn and Andrea started swerving back and forth down 1960 headed east. Heading towards Marilyn's, David turns on her street and pulls into the corner store. Next pulls up Marilyn, then Andrea. Marilyn parks and gets out to confront Andrea.

Banging on the windows, Marilyn yells for Andrea to get out of the car. Before Andrea opens the door, David jumps between the door and Marilyn. "Don't beat her ass right here!" and points at Angel in the back-seat sleep. "Bitch, you lucky baby girl in the back seat. I got you though." That was just one occurrence that should have been enough to make Marilyn walk away from him. But she didn't. Despite the issues he had with the mother of his daughter,

David seemed to be a good guy; the kind that you could settle down and have kids with. Over the next month, Marilyn decided to let David meet Caleb.

Sitting outside of Marilyn's apartment, David sat watching Caleb on his skateboard. "Say, lil' man! Whatcha you got there?" David asks Caleb.

Caleb yells out, "My skateboard! You wanna see a cool trick?"

"Of course! Let me see what you got!" Caleb takes off and does a *cool trick* on his skateboard.

As Marilyn is laughing, she attempts to call Caleb over to introduce the two of them when David yells to Caleb, "Aye, I can do a cool trick too. Let me see that skateboard." Caleb hands the skateboard to David.

David tries to hit a trick but hits the ground instead. They all laughed loudly and uncontrollably. "Man! Let me get my big ass somewhere and sit down." David says. "This lil ass skateboard got my ass hurting!" They all laugh some more. Marilyn's mom comes home from work and sees them outside. As she's getting out of her car to go in the house, Caleb runs to greet her. While hugging him, she stops and says "Well, hello! I'm Marilyn's mom, Ms. Smith. Who are you?" with her hand held out for a handshake.

While gripping her hand firmly, "Hello ma'am! I'm David! A friend of Marilyn's. How you doing?"

"Okay! I like the way you grabbed my hand. Let's me know you're a real man and not these lil boys she's used to playing with. I'm doing good! Thanks for asking."

Marilyn rolls her eyes and twists her lips all in one motion. "Nice to meet you too, ma'am! Have a nice day." David responds.

Marilyn rolls her eyes again as her mom is walking off. "So glad I was able to introduce y'all!" Marilyn says sarcastically to David as he begins to laugh.

"Y'all wild man! But it's cool. I know who I am. That didn't bother me." David turns his attention back to Caleb ``Say, buddy! Next time I come over here, I'ma bring you a real skateboard. Cool?" David tells Caleb.

"Cool!" Caleb responds and takes off again. "Aight Marilyn, I gotta run and go get my baby. I may swing back by, if not, I'll definitely be calling you." He leans in and gives Marilyn a kiss on her cheek.

"Okay, David! Tell baby girl I said hey and can't wait to see her again."

"Sure thing!" As David leaves, Marilyn and Caleb take a walk to the mailbox. In the mail, there's a letter from Vernon. Marilyn's eyes widened and her heart began to race as she hurried back to the apartment to open it.

* * *

"To my Tootie! Here's a poem that I wanted to share with you that describes how I feel about you my love. It's called 'Perfect Love, Perfect Friend'," writes Vernon.

Because you are my love, I know the joy that comes from feeling closer to someone than I've ever felt before. Because you are my love, I know the passion of wanting to share everything I have, everything I am with you and only you.

Because you are my friend, I know that I can count on you to hold my hand through the rough times and to be there to share the good times, too.

Because you are my friend, I'll always have someone to make me smile; just when I need it most, to encourage me when I'm feeling confused or doubtful.

And I know that I must be one of the luckiest people in the world to have someone like you-the perfect love, the perfect friend.

Baby girl, you mean the world to me and I promise to always cherish you. I love you, my love bug. Infinity LOVE, Always MINE, Forever YOURS. Vernon, "The Truth"

After reading that poem, all Marilyn could do was smile from ear to ear, but the guilt of falling for David had begun to set in. She then begins to wonder how she would tell Vernon or if she ever would. He would be heartbroken! Marilyn couldn't live with hurting Vernon, so she decided to wait a bit longer especially since she and David weren't actually dating yet. Marilyn would soon see and understand the kind of man David was. One that she didn't have to worry about his ability or desire to take care of his responsibilities. He would do it proudly.

One day, while on the phone with Marilyn, David could hear her and her mother getting into it about her refund check and he could hear Marilyn leaving the house. "Man, you alright over there? Where are you going? Do I need to come get you and Caleb?" David asks.

"I'm good, that's her! It's all good. The cops on the way! I bet she gone unassed my money today and when she does, Caleb and I are GONE!" Marilyn responds. The cops pull up and after hearing both sides, Ms. Smith agreed to give Marilyn all her money back the next day but wanted her to get her things and get out.

"That's fine with me! Caleb and I were leaving anyway. Thank you, Officer!" Marilyn goes into the house to pack a few things to leave.

"Girl, where you gone go?" asks David.

"Hell, if I know. More than likely, we will be in the Intown Suites right down the street. That'll hold us for a week until I figure things out." Marilyn responds.

"Oh hell naw! I know what it's like having to live in a motel. That's all Intown Suites is. I will not sit back and let you or Caleb go there. Let me talk to my Grandpa to see if y'all can come here." David responds. "Meanwhile, I'm about to come get y'all because I know she aint gone let you use her car now."

Marilyn sits there with Caleb waiting for David. Thirty minutes later, he pulls up and they head to his grandpa's house. "Now, I talked to my grandpa and he's okay with y'all coming to stay for a while until you can get on your feet. Don't worry about paying for anything, I got it!" David tells Marilyn.

"Are you sure? I appreciate that!" Marilyn responds.

"Yeah, it's no problem. In fact, you're the first girl my Grandpa has ever liked. He's always asking where his "buddy" Caleb is. Anyway, you know I've been trying to catch up with my mama so I can introduce y'all. Since we're together and all, we are about to go see her now."

"Together huh?!" Marilyn smiles. "Oh, Lord! Hope she doesn't do me like my mama did you!"

They both started laughing. "Nah, she aight!"

They pull up to where his mom is and not only does Marilyn and Caleb meet David's mama, but they also meet his Big Mama and his mama's husband. "Hey, mama! This is Marilyn and her son Caleb."

"Hey Marilyn! How are you?"

"I'm fine and yourself?"

"I'm doing good! Who is this cute lil' fella?"

"This is my son, Caleb! He's 5 years old."

"Oh ok! He's a few years older than Angel!" David mama responds.

"Yep!" says David.

"Well y'all come on in the house. Big Mama wants to see you!"

"Mama, you know I'm coming in. That nigga in there?"

"Now, Jr., don't start that shit now!"

David laughs. "You know I gotta ask. You know I don't like that nigga, but because I love me some Big Mama, that fool get a pass!"

His mama throws her hands up. They all walk in the house to see and meet Big Mama. After meeting everybody, David, Marilyn, and Caleb leave to head to his grandpa's house.

* * *

The next day, Marilyn gets the rest of her money from her mama along with the rest of her things to move in with David and his grandpa. After about six months of living together at his grandpa house, David and Marilyn decide to get an apartment together. While going through all those changes, Marilyn had begun to slack off with writing Vernon but did find the time to write Vernon to tell him that she was seeing someone. Because she had a key to the mailbox, she would use David's car to go check the mail every day and the letter she had been dreading was there waiting to be read.

"Marilyn, I want you to know that I'm fucked up with your decision to move on and start seeing someone else. I kind of figured that when our communication wasn't as strong as it normally is. All I gotta say to that is just don't get pregnant! I'm smart enough to understand that you would eventually start seeing somebody since I'm not there. I prepared myself for that and me not being there makes it easier for you. Just please don't get pregnant! I love you, Marilyn. Always have and always will.
Vernon, "Your Truth"

Marilyn broke down crying because she was already pregnant. The main reason David and Marilyn decided to move in their own spot was because they found out that she was pregnant. David was excited after sharing with Marilyn that he and his baby mama had lost their son. Little did she know, David had also shared their pregnancy news with Andrea. That started more drama and that excitement would be short-lived. Some kind of way, Andrea got Marilyn's number and would play on her phone.

"Damn, bitch! What you want and why the hell you keep playing on my damn phone?"

Marilyn knew it was her because she blocked her number, but Andrea would still call private.

"So I heard y'all pregnant?"

"How the hell would you know that? That ain't your business!"

"Jr. told me and I have been in y'all new apartment!" Andrea shared.

Marilyn was pissed and felt betrayed. Right as David was pulling up, he could hear Marilyn yelling and screaming on the phone. "You stupid ass bitch, what the fuck you doing in my house while I'm at work? You dumb ass broad..."

David walks up and grabs the phone to see who it is. "Hello?!

Man, why you calling with that dumb shit?" apparently she was in the middle of saying something because he said "Bitch, fuck you!" and hung up.

They are now back in the apartment. Marilyn is crying and screaming. "Why the fuck you had that bitch in our apartment?" Marilyn asks.

"Man, I only had her ass in here to show her what she is missing out on and how good you have it! We didn't do anything! I put that on my son. Her ass just mad that I will never stick my shit back in her dirty ass." says David. Marilyn didn't want to believe him, but she did, however, that moment begin to build up a wall.

"Man, I swear I can't stand her ass and pray for the day to lay these hands on her. Fuck!" Marilyn lets out an aching scream and runs to the toilet. "Oh my God! I'm bleeding! Lord, please let the baby be okay!" Marilyn pleads.

"You want me to call the doctor?" David asks.

"Yes! Call right now to see what we need to do." Marilyn responds.

David gets the doctor on the phone; they ask for Marilyn. "Hello! Yes. There's a bad, aching pain in my stomach and I'm sitting on the toilet bleeding! Okay, I will. See you all tomorrow!" Marilyn hangs up with her doctor.

"Well, what did they say? David asks.

Marilyn gets up to wipe herself and notices a red substance with something tiny inside shaped like a 4 to 6-week-old embryo. Marilyn knew right then and there that she had miscarried yet again but was still prayerful that she didn't until getting to the doctor tomorrow. "They said for me to lie down and rest and that I need to come to the doctor first thing in the morning. I'm going to go lay down. You can do whatever it is you were going to do. I'm done talking to you!" Marilyn lays down and immediately starts to cry. Not only does she know that she just miscarried, but she also misses the hell out of Vernon and wants to tell him so badly about the pregnancy, and what happened.

* * *

The next morning at the doctor, the results came back that Marilyn, in fact, had a miscarriage and that everything had passed on its own; no D&C would be needed. Marilyn and David leave the doctor's office and arrive back home.

"Okay baby! I'ma let you get some rest and head to the studio."

"The studio? WE JUST LOST OUR BABY BEHIND YOUR STUPID ASS BABY MAMA and all you're worried about is a studio? Bye, David!"

David didn't try to explain, he just left. Marilyn cried and cried until she couldn't cry no more thinking, "Vernon wouldn't act this way!" While David is gone, she decides to write Vernon to tell him.

"Hey, my love! First, I'm so sorry! I love you so much and missing you the same. You know that we have NEVER kept anything from each other, so it's killing me to tell you this now. I was pregnant, but I lost the baby behind some stupid ass shit with David and his baby mama. I'm so sorry and pray you don't turn your back on me. No matter what I do out here, you will ALWAYS have a place in my heart. No one can or will ever take your place in my heart. I love you so much. I really do! I hope and pray you find it in your heart to forgive me. I LOVE YOU ALWAYS.
Perfect love, Perfect friend
Your Tootie"

For the next few weeks, the tension would become steady between David and Marilyn. The smallest thing David did made Marilyn angry and they would argue all the time. She couldn't understand why David had shown little to no feelings about losing their baby.

One day, Marilyn decided to ask. "David, we need to talk!"

"What's up?" David responded.

"I need to know why aren't you acknowledging the fact that we aren't with child anymore? Also, that it's you and your sad ass baby mama fault?"

Before Marilyn can go any further, David stops her. "Because I don't have any emotions behind that. After losing my son, my feelings of disappointment became numb. I don't know what to do, so I stay away to not have to deal with it."

Marilyn looks at him with a stupid look. She walks away into the bedroom. David follows behind her. "Baby, I'm sorry! I really am. I don't know what to do. What do you need me to do?" David asks.

"I want you to leave me alone!" she responds. Instead of listening and granting her request, David did what he would always do to make Marilyn forget about the argument they had. Sexual healing. For the next month, Marilyn would go to work, pick up Caleb from school, come home, cook, wash up, go to bed, and do it all over the next day...without saying a word to David. She too became numb and the wall continued to build.

Things became so dry that David decided it would be best for them to separate from each other for a while and to move back into his grandpa's house to figure things out. He was gone for about two months, but in that time, David would come by to "chill" with Marilyn and Caleb.

* * *

It is now December 2009 and although David and Marilyn are still "not back together", Marilyn hit David with some exciting news. "Hey, baby! What you doin'?" Marilyn asks David.

"Nothing! Chillin' over her at Pa' house. What's up?" David responds.

"Guess what?"

"What?!" They go back and forward for a second playing the guessing game.

"No crazy!! We're pregnant again!!!" Marilyn tells David.

"You lying?" David responds. Marilyn begins to laugh and cry at the same time.

"No, I'm not! I've been feeling sick and decided to take a pregnancy test. We are pregnant again!" says Marilyn.

"Hell naw! I'm so happy! Baby, I'm coming home."

Within a week, David was back home. Things were smooth sailing between the two of them. Of course, there were issues still arising between David and Andrea, but Marilyn decided that she would stay out of their mess to keep from beating Andrea's ass and to make sure their baby was growing. During this time, Marilyn wrote Vernon to tell him. He wasn't too thrilled about it, but he never talked down on her and always made sure that her feelings were put before his when expressing his feelings.

Eventually, things would turn for the worst yet again and Marilyn would start back confiding in Vernon. One day, when Marilyn got off work, she went to go see Vernon. Pregnant and all. Vernon was transferred to the Central Unit for a class he was taking and to be closer to Marilyn. Once he was settled, he called to inform her of his move.

Marilyn is sitting in the Central Prison Unit Visitation Room when she notices her man Vernon coming out. She's blushing and so is he. Sitting behind the glass, Vernon tells Marilyn to stand up. She does. He then shakes his head at her and Marilyn puts her head down. "Cheer up, my love! Although I'm hurt and fucked up, I still love you!" That put a huge smile on Marilyn's face. They continued to talk for two hours before Marilyn had to leave. Marilyn began to cry because she didn't want to leave him there. "Baby, wipe your face!" Vernon tries to comfort her from behind the glass. "Everything will be okay! Although I'm not there physically, I'm still right there and you're still right here." Vernon points to both of their hearts. "That'll never change. Trust." Vernon assures Marilyn. They press their hands on the glass signifying the love and intimacy they share.

While on the way home, Marilyn thought to herself, "I can't believe this man is still willing to accept me as his woman although I'm pregnant!" That moment would define how deep Marilyn's love for Vernon goes. Deeply in love.

* * *

Making it back home, the internal vibe wasn't there but Marilyn's entanglement to David was based on having a security blanket and to keep up the façade of a picture-perfect family. As family-oriented people, David and Marilyn wanted the Huxtable life; mom and dad in the same house raising children. It was something they both craved from childhood even though they knew they were better off as friends. The love for each other was there, but not the kind that is passionate and life-changing. Life going forward would prove this to be true.

CHAPTER 4

BUTTERFLY MAGIC

Throughout the course of Marilyn's *courtship* with David, the rollercoaster ride became a tradition. After giving birth to their first daughter, Rai'lyn, things were great. David was in love with her and would not let her out his sight. Marilyn didn't have to do anything but rest because David wanted to do it all. Literally. He felt this was his second chance at fatherhood since he was robbed of that with his first daughter, Angel.

Marilyn would soon tell Vernon about the birth of Rai'lyn as he wanted to see pictures of her. Marilyn losing her job and David's income not being enough to cover all the bills alone caused them to move back with David's grandpa. That started to become a hectic environment due to David's messy ass family. David would be sure to get them back into their own place as he was getting sick of his family having something to say about him and Marilyn living there with *her two kids*. His family would soon get the best of Marilyn and she would wait for the perfect time to go in on all of them. Except she wouldn't have to say a word because David said he would take care of it all.

"So, we are calling a family meeting because there are things that are going on over here at Pa's house and we don't like it!" says the oldest aunt. David, his mom, the oldest aunt, her husband, his Grandpa, and one male cousin was there. Marilyn is in the back room listening as David didn't want her to be in there because he had it covered. At least that's what he thought. "Jr, we don't like that you have that girl, her son, and now another baby living here. You all don't pay no bills here, no groceries, barely keeping things clean because her son has his toys all over the place. It's time for y'all to go!" His mom standing there not saying a word made David even angrier.

As he was in the middle of addressing his oldest Aunt, Marilyn couldn't hold it any longer. She came out the back room so fast, David couldn't move quick enough to stop her. "First of all, you old hag, if you have ANYTHING to say about me or my children, ADDRESS ME, BITCH! You got the right one! Grandpa, please forgive me for my language, but you old bat, I'm bout sicka you! Your ass is the only one that always got something to say. It's my damn food stamp card that's buying ALL the groceries. You wouldn't know that because your fat ass baby sister is always coming over here taking shit back to her house, but then again, you all know that because she was stealing shit from over here way before I even knew David according to Mama. David and I keep this damn house clean. A FEW toys here and there does not mean the house is dirty. Hell, it was ME that cleaned both the front and back room, while David was at work, that was filthy as hell BEFORE my son and I moved in here the first time. Oh, and another thing, I haven't seen nan one of y'all over here YET to make sure Pa is okay or cooking for him. Maybe because y'all only come over to be nosy. However, it's David and I that's making sure he's good and eating the way he's supposed to with occasional Jack in the Box, if that's what he wants. SO, MISS ME WITH THAT BULLSHIT you talking. One more thing, YOU don't have to worry about me and mine cause, bitch, we outta this hellhole as soon as our apartment is ready and none of y'all bet not touch my shit while I'm gone!"

Marilyn grabs her purse and leaves. "It takes one to know one, bitch!" says his aunt. Marilyn turns around. "Bitch, fuck you!" Marilyn turns back around and walks out the burglar bar. She could hear David tell his mom, "Mama, you and I gon talk cause you fucking up! Matter of fact, fuck all y'all! Pa, I love you and I'll be back. Call me if you need me!" David and Marilyn leave to go get the kids from Marilyn's mom.

The car ride was silent. Marilyn was pissed and was sick of David's aunt. David didn't realize it, but her wall was building rapidly. She was changing. A heavy burden was starting to weigh her down. She couldn't stand his mama's side of the family. She started to hate them. Marilyn couldn't wait to write Vernon about this bullshit.

It wasn't until 2011 when Marilyn became pregnant with their second baby girl, Marie, that she was in constant contact with Vernon. Sneaking on the phone at night, taking her time coming home from work just to have another 30 minutes on the phone and on the nights that David was out all night. Marilyn was so bold and became carefree with talking to Vernon on the constant that she, one night while lying on the couch across from a sleeping David, talked to Vernon all night.

Marilyn didn't realize it, but he heard her whispering on the phone. Less than thrilled about it, David brought it up to Marilyn and no matter how much they argued about it. Marilyn wasn't going to stop until she was ready, if ever, and there was absolutely NOTHING David could do about it. Vernon was Marilyn's safe haven, best friend, confidant, and most importantly, her soulmate and absolutely nobody was going to take that away from her. The roller coaster tradition of a relationship that David and Marilyn were in stayed the same. Happy times, bad times, hard times, repeat!

✳ ✳ ✳

It is now February 2013 and Marilyn is right at 8 months pregnant with their baby boy, King David. Everyone is asleep in bed and Marilyn gets up to use the bathroom. She hears David's phone going off repeatedly. She grabs it and reads the text messages coming through from an unknown number. "Hey, you! Last night was good! Can't wait until the next time." Marilyn grows furious and wakes David up. He comes into the bathroom with her. "What's up, baby? Everything okay?" Marilyn doesn't say a word. She just hands him the phone. He looks at it and cries, "Baby, I'm sorry!" Marilyn threw her hands up in the motion of *I don't want to hear it* and gave him the *niggas aint shit!!* look. Instead of trying to talk, David left the bathroom and Marilyn began to cry.

He could hear her crying and attempted to talk again but she wasn't listening. In one ear and out the other. Marilyn felt so low, but her wall was steadily rising, keeping David on the other side. She wished that at that very second that Vernon would call and tell her he's outside. She would've gladly grabbed her shit and left. Pregnant and all. Only thing is, she never told Vernon that she was pregnant again. In her mind, she was disappointing him and hated when he was hurt.

The next morning, after taking Caleb to school, Rai'lyn and Marie to daycare, David came back home. Marilyn went in on him. "So about last night and that bullshit I read. I just want to know two things. Why did you do it and would you have done it again had I not saw the messages?" Because David and Marilyn never lied to each other, whether by admission or finding out, David replied, "I cheated because you were never in the mood this time to give me some. And yes, had you not seen the messages, I would've done it again!"

Marilyn slapped the shit outta David and stood there waiting on his reaction (the last time she did that, David slapped her back and afterwards, Marilyn started punching him until he grabbed her to calm her down). Instead, David walked away to get ready for work. Marilyn started crying again. David left for work but tried to apologize again. Marilyn cried some more and started cleaning up to keep her mind off the bs she just heard. Thinking about Vernon and wishing he could save her from the hell she was in, she cried some more. David called to check on her, but all he could hear was screaming, cussing, and then the dial tone. A few hours later, Marilyn's water broke! She called David to tell him. He damn near flew home and was in a panic. Marilyn, not bothered at all, made her way to the truck, not wanting to be touched by David.

* * *

They get to the hospital and David is nervous. Not because his son is about to be born, but because he's not sure if Marilyn wants him to be near her while giving birth. Marilyn never said a word to David and the tension was thick in the room between them. Marilyn's mom sensed something so to keep her out of their business, Marilyn broke. "David, why are you standing way over there? Come get your first-born son. He's all yours!" David gave Marilyn that "Are you sure?" look before coming near her to hold King David. The tension lessoned and they were all smiling. Little did David know, Marilyn was still pissed and really didn't want his ass there, but she knew THIS moment, with his first-born boy, meant so much to him.

* * *

Back home from the hospital, King David is bundled up sleeping. Marilyn must take a bath sitting down to ease the tension down below since she was torn. Although she went into early labor, King was 7 lbs and did a little damage coming out. David is standing outside the door listening to Marilyn crying. He comes in and Marilyn wipes her face. "What do you want? Your son is in *there* sleeping!" Marilyn says to David.

"Well, I know that, but his mother is in *here* crying because of me and I don't like it. I want to talk!" he responds.

"Well you should've thought about how I would feel before sticking your dick in another woman. I'm good and really don't want to talk about it!" snaps Marilyn.

David attempts to help Marilyn wash. She gestures that she doesn't need his help, but David knew better and kept helping. Marilyn obliged. Standing there allowing David to bathe her, Marilyn had Vernon on her mind and began to cry some more. Poor David thinking it was still solely because of his actions, he started to console Marilyn. She cried even more.

For the next year, things were okay between David and Marilyn, However, she continued to talk to Vernon whenever she was away from David and although she never told him upfront about King David, he knew she was keeping something from him.

"Hey, my love! What's going on? You haven't been yourself when we talk. Everything ok out there?" Vernon asked.

"Yes, Vernon! Everything is okay! Why do you keep asking me that?" Marilyn responds.

"Well because I know you. You don't pull back from talking to me unless something is going on. Are you pregnant again?" Marilyn knew right then and there that she had to be honest. She never lied to Vernon and was not about to start now.

With a deep sigh, Marilyn replied, "No Vernon, I'm not pregnant again."

Vernon cuts her off, "Then, what's up my love? What's going on out there? Something is bothering you. I can feel it!"

"VERNON!!" Marilyn speaks loudly to get his attention.

"Yes, my love!"

"Like I was saying, I'm not pregnant BUT I was and didn't want to hurt you, so I didn't say anything. I gave birth to my handsome son, King David." Marilyn tells Vernon.

He gets really quiet. A hot five minutes went by before he said another word. "Really Marilyn? I know I can't stop you from having relations with this man. I'm in here, but really? I don't know what to say." Vernon is hurt, and Marilyn doesn't know what to say.

"Marilyn, I love you! I really love you. I'm in love with you and want you to be my wife. You know this and have known this way before you met David. I just want you to realize that. I have nothing against your babies because they didn't ask to be here. I don't even fault this man. **You** are responsible for this. The things you share with me about y'all relationship has me thinking y'all aren't working but then you keep getting pregnant! This is crazy." Marilyn still doesn't know what to say. Vernon was right! She knew her season with David was up before it even started but she did not have the courage to leave, especially with four kids now.

* * *

The day is approaching for Vernon's 31st birthday and Marilyn is planning to go see him. That would be a 3 ½ hour drive since he was done with school and had to go back to his original unit. Marilyn didn't mind. She was going to see her baby, and nothing was going to stop her. Marilyn calls up Nicole to do her hair and to have her ride up there with her. "So, girl, you want me to ride up here to see Vernon? What is it with you two? Y'all still rocking after all these years? You must really love this negro! What the hell did you tell David?" says Nicole.

"I absolutely love him!" Marilyn says proudly as she begins to blush. "This is why I need you to ride with me. This will be my first time driving that far. And I didn't tell him anything yet! Don't really have to."

"Well you know I'm down to go see my brother. It's about time and I know he's mad I haven't written him in a while." says Nicole. They start laughing. "But yeah, I'll ride with you."

"Cool!"

* * *

Vernon's birthday is here, and Marilyn is preparing to leave when David asks her where she was going. "I'm about to leave and I'll be back later tonight. I need a break! Nicole and I will be together." Marilyn replies.

"Hell nah! When y'all two hang, it's always some sneaky shit going on! Where the hell are you going? You think I'm stupid, I know that nigga birthday today and you got me fucked up if you think you about to drive the car I got you to go see this nigga. Matter of fact, you ain't going no motherfucking where. Better sit your ass down!" David shouts.

"First off, you're right! I'm not going in the car WE bought, I got a rental. And I AM going to go see him. You can't stop me. We aren't married!" They get into a quick scuffle over the keys and eventually, David throws them and says, "Fuck you, bitch! Go see that bird looking ass nigga then and when you get back, yo shit gone be outside!"

Marilyn laughs to herself but responds just as vicious. "Fuck me? Nah, bitch. Fuck YOU! This right here is EXACTLY why I'm going to go see that bird looking ass nigga. The same bird looking ass nigga that values the woman I am. And I promise you my shit better be in the same place I left it when I get back." Marilyn responds while walking off.

"I don't know why you think I won't beat yo ass playing with me. You lucky the kids here." David tells her.

"Nigga, please. You weren't gon do shit even if they weren't here. Do I look like your baby mama? The fuck no." Marilyn replied as she walked out the door and slammed it.

As she was getting in the car, David came out running after her to drag her back in the house. Marilyn laughed, put the rental in reverse and left. "FUCK YOU, BITCH!!" Marilyn could hear David yell out as she pulled out the gate. It didn't bother her, she was going to go see the one who kept a smile on her face, her Vernon! Nothing and no one else mattered. While picking up Nicole, David is blowing Marilyn up nonstop! She never answers because she's laughing and giggling with Vernon. "Did he hit you? Cause I'll have somebody knocking on that door real quick like before." says Vernon. Vernon had one of his homeboys do a popup at Marilyn's door because she hadn't written him.

"Not at all! We were just scuffling over the keys and he threw them thinking I wouldn't find them. Anyway, none of that matters. I'm on my way to see you." Marilyn tells Vernon.

Marilyn and Nicole arrive at the unit. After going through all the extra security, Marilyn and Nicole are given a phone booth to sit at. Vernon comes out smiling extra hard. Marilyn can't even look him in the eyes without crying and smiling at the same time. She hadn't seen him since 2010 and it is now 2014. Those 2 hours seemed like a lifetime of smiles and tears from them both. Nicole left and went to the car for the remaining time. As the time winds down for them to leave, Vernon tells Marilyn that he loves her. Marilyn responds, but is sad to leave him there.

* * *

On the way back home, while talking to Vernon, Marilyn couldn't help but think about David and what he was up to. "Ain't no telling what he is doing. Probably chillin' with that baby mama of his. I don't care as long as he didn't touch my shit." Marilyn thinks to herself. "Alright Vernon, I made it back home. I love you and happy birthday again baby! I love you so much."

"I love you too baby girl! Thank you for coming to see me for my birthday. Now, don't go in there arguing with him. Not worth it!" says Vernon.

"Trust me I'm not! I'm going straight in here to take a shower and go to bed. I love you."

"Okay baby! Good night!"

"Good night."

Marilyn walks in the house and surprisingly, David was cool and was cutting Caleb's hair. Marilyn didn't say a word. David comes in the room behind her and closes the door. "Well, I'm glad you made it back safely. I have a question. What is it about this nigga? What is he doing that I'm not doing because clearly, he is doing something. Y'all had a baby or something together? This nigga got you wrapped around his shit or voodoo or something?" Marilyn didn't answer any of those questions. David became irritated that she didn't respond but he did not react. David would never know that she miscarried with Vernon as well. Vernon still didn't know. "So, since you won't answer those questions, answer this one and I'll leave you alone. Was that visit behind the glass or was it contact?" asked David.

Growing irritated, Marilyn knew where this was going, "No David, the visit was not contact. I could only talk to him from behind the glass." She rolls her eyes and walks off, but not before seeing that dumb ass smirk on his face. "As long as you didn't have

50

that contact visit, I'm good." Marilyn paid David no mind because she knew he was being petty.

* * *

Months passed and assuming David forgave her and was ready to settle down, Marilyn's communication with Vernon began to somewhat take a back seat. She started giving more of her attention to David, especially when the talk of marriage came up. This is something they both wanted. Husband and wife with their kids living happily after ever. David and Marilyn dated for five years. He proposed to her in October of 2014 and got married on December 13, 2014. The planning process was hectic and was nowhere near the dream Marilyn had. Marilyn and her mother got into it because she wasn't excited like a mother should be. She told David and Marilyn "If y'all get married before me, I'm going to be upset!"

Marilyn acted as if that didn't bother her by laughing it off, but David knew it messed her up. Not only did it mess her up, but her mom proved her words to be true. She came in at the very end to help get things done....after Marilyn had to cry about it and seeing that Marilyn's Bonus Mom, Denise, was stepping up making sure Marilyn had the things that she and David could afford in such short notice. Before they could get married, they went through marriage counseling. While talking to Pastor Lamont, the main and only thing David wanted to be sure of was that Marilyn was over Vernon and Marilyn wanted to make sure David was done with flirting and cheating. They both said yes, and BOTH were lying.

The day would come for Marilyn to get married. It's time to walk down the aisle and as soon as the song starts, Marilyn walks in and bursts into tears. The guests think she's crying because it's her wedding day, but she's crying because she hears Vernon's voice in her head telling her not to do it. The day would go on and everything was cool and went according to plan. It's time to go and David has to meet Andrea on their wedding night to bring Angel back since his mama left early because she wasn't feeling good. Marilyn was irritated that she had to see this girl on her wedding day. *Now, why the hell I gotta see this hoe on my wedding day? I can't have shit without her whack ass presence being around.* Marilyn says to herself.

* * *

Two months after their honeymoon, Marilyn and David are pregnant with their last baby girl, Simone. This pregnancy would prove to be the hardest. Marilyn was hospitalized due to shortness of breath from pulmonary embolisms. She would then be placed on blood thinners throughout the entire pregnancy. David made sure Marilyn was good as he did when Rai'lyn was born. David was a great father to all 6 of his kids. Caleb included. However, Simone brought David and Marilyn a bit closer. She would also bring Vernon and Marilyn closer. Marilyn sent Vernon pictures of Simone and not only did she capture his heart, he started calling her *his* baby. David would never find out about that. Ever.

CHAPTER 5

EMOTIONAL WARFARE

After getting married, Marilyn still decided to not cut off contact with Vernon. She just couldn't do it. She loved David, but never really knew if she was *in* love with him. Eventually, she told David that she was going to let Vernon go. **That was a lie.** She thought if she said it out loud, maybe she'd truly be able to let go of him. But her heart was still attached to Vernon and she couldn't shake him. On several occasions, during the intimate moments between her and David, Marilyn would picture that it was Vernon and would sing like a canary. As time progressed, she didn't want to keep lying to David. He didn't deserve that. David thought that she and Vernon just had a friendship. What he didn't know was she and Vernon were in love.

The difficult part was telling him. They'd been married for two years before she gathered up the nerve to tell him. Their marriage went downhill from there. Marilyn spent all those years hiding her true feelings from David. She struggled with herself about her feelings for Vernon. She often thought, *"How can I be in love with someone who isn't here?"* Sometimes it didn't make sense in her mind. But she knew she loved him and couldn't anybody convince her otherwise. Marilyn thought that if she focused on David, who was there providing and taking care of her and their children, that she would be absolved of her feelings for Vernon. She figured she had better put her *all* into loving the man that was loving her physically.

It took her a while, but she managed to convince herself, yet again, that David is whom she was supposed to be with. Although she married David, her heart was with Vernon. It wasn't right, but she settled for a life with David only because she couldn't have Vernon the way she wanted him. Vernon and Marilyn kept in contact on and off throughout her marriage. David's knowledge of them keeping in contact caused more problems for them. Marilyn's heart was dedicated to someone who was not her husband. She would become torn between two men. This left Marilyn feeling guilty a lot. The internal struggle declared war within her. She went back and forth with herself and couldn't fully remove herself from either of them. Marilyn had a different experience with each of them, one that bonded different sides of her to them.

There were times when she'd tell Vernon that her marriage wasn't working out and she wanted to make things work with him. Then she'd pull back from him to try and give David her all because she loved him and took an oath under God with her vows. Marilyn's behavior confused and frustrated both men. She was confused too. This was something she tried hard to mask for the sake of love.

CHAPTER 6
THE FINAL STRAW

It is now May 2018. David and Marilyn are now just about done with each other but are still hanging in there for the kids. Marilyn decides to join a motorcycle social club that her friend Crystal introduced her to. David was 100% against that environment because of the unwanted drama that it normally leads to. In this situation, David was right and for a whole year, Marilyn would participate actively. That meant she would be up early in the morning for community service or out all night at events supporting other social clubs or the motorcycle set as a whole.

She was barely home in between work, school, church, and the social club. She would even begin to get close to TGG, a gentleman with the set. Confusion at its finest. All of this was the final straw for David and the ultimatum of leaving the club or divorce was up in the air. He didn't really want a divorce but wanted her to see how serious he was about leaving the set. See, Marilyn doesn't like ultimatums, so she wrote "fuck no" in red on each paper that came through the fax machine, sent it back the same way those divorce papers came, and she stayed in the club. Deep down, Marilyn knew the set life was not for her. However, the set allowed her to "live freely" in a sense.

She and David would go back and forth for a while behind the set lifestyle. That caused them to grow even further apart. Marilyn was still writing and talking to Vernon as well and received a card from him. She'd hope it would be the response to her telling him about the miscarriage she had and that the baby was his.

My thoughts: Baby girl I'm just sitting here with you in my thoughts and beating in my heart. My thoughts are remembering the first time I kissed you. Remembering the very first hug. Remembering the first time we made love!! Just thoughts of everything with you. From day one, I knew that you would be a blessing to my life and vice versa. Right now, I'm just under the weather of my feelings. Just trying to be strong about some things. But lately, it has been nothing but thunderstorms with my emotions and feelings. I chase these clouds, and thunderstorms away by thinking of you, which gives me partial calm and peace when I most need it. I love you baby girl, I really do!!

I'm happy to know that we actually conceived but sad that you went through that and didn't let me know so I can at least be there for you. I understand your reasoning, but I love you and it was my duty to make sure you were okay. Baby, I'm just waiting on my moment so that I can give you all the joy you give to me!! Every day since I first met you I have been carrying your heart. I carry it in my heart. I am never without it. Anywhere I go, you go. For you, but-terfly, are my world. I pray that you have smiled knowing my truth about you because you are my truth. The fact of our relationship will always remain the same; nobody would ever be able to come between the fact that we belong together. Always mine, forever yours. Vernon, The Truth.
PS. My love and loyalty are bulletproof and don't you ever forget that.
#WaitingOnOurMoment

Reading that card made Marilyn miss Vernon even more.

* * *

In 2019, David and Marilyn pretty much accepted that they were at their rope's end. David started going out more and Marilyn was starting to stay home, but Vernon was also at the end of his rope with Marilyn. Another card came and Marilyn knew he would be feeling some type of way.

February 3, 2019 12:10 PM
My thoughts: Just sitting here thinking I haven't received a piece of mail from you since September of last year. "SMH" That's totally unacceptable!! I keep asking myself "Vernon, why would you allow Marilyn to treat you this way when you have been nothing but 1,000 with her?" My conclusion to that is "she's only going to do what you allow her to do." I'm tired of my heart being drugged along because I want to be loved. If you can't love me like you promised you would, then let me go. Stop stringing me along like it's going to be all about me when you know it's not. All I wanted was just to be able to connect with you.

I'm afraid I have lost the connection. I love you Marilyn always have, always will! You know my heart, you know my soul, you know me! I'm not turning my back on you, I'm just telling you the truth! And you know what the truth is between us! I know you love me. I can't deny that, but what is best for us at this moment? I have two years left until my moment of freedom. You already know what it is on my end. I don't know when you'll read this and I don't know where my life might be, but this is my truth to you. The loneliest place in the world is the human heart especially when love is absent. I will hope you understand that and I hope to hear from you soon. If not, just know you will always remain in my heart always mine, forever yours
Vernon, The Truth.

Marilyn would never write back.

CHAPTER 7

SECRETS OF THE DEAD

April 6, 2019. It was Marie's last cheer competition of the season in San Marcos. David and Marilyn left home early that morning to get there around 10 am. A few of the other parents from the squad did the same thing. They would all make it down there with time to spare to sit down for breakfast. David, Marilyn, the assistant team mom (Marilyn was the head Team Mom), her boyfriend, their daughter and Marie all went to Denny's. They are all seated inside when David gets up to go to the restroom. On his way back, the assistant gets up to go to the restroom. She and David cross each other and start to laugh. Marilyn thinks nothing of it because the assistant is a "Becky" in a black girl's body and David gave the "Excuse me! You're in my way!" kind of look. She comes back, they all eat and leave to head to the competition.

The vibe between Marilyn and David was off and that wasn't normal especially when it comes to something dealing with the kids. The tension was thick, and everyone noticed. Marilyn leaves to go to the car to cool off. David never followed. She sends him a long text. He never responds. So she walks back in, and as she's walking in she sees Becky, the assistant, walking back in and hears her whisper in his ear, "You look better when you smile." Marilyn still didn't think nothing of it because Becky was friendly and did others the same way. It is now time for the Cyclones to perform. David is nowhere to be found so Marilyn texts him. He comes from around the corner.

Competition is over and the girls win second place. Pictures are taken, everybody says their goodbyes, especially Becky, the assistant. She yells out her window, "Make sure you all let us know when you make it home!"

Marilyn responds, "Okay girl! Talk to you later." They all leave. Marilyn gets comfortable and tries to hold David's hand. He pulls away. "Bai, what's wrong with you?" Her intuition is telling her something is wrong.

"Nothing, I'm good! Just don't want to hold hands right now."

"Well, that's strange! You never NOT want to hold my hand especially when we're on these long road trips. But okay! I'm taking a nap. Wake me up to take over driving when you need me to." Marilyn wasn't bothered at all. To sleep she went. Halfway home, Marilyn wakes up to take over because she could feel them drifting. They stop at Whataburger to get something to eat before heading back on the road again. This time, David is in the mood to hold hands. Marilyn doesn't pull away immediately, but eventually does when he falls asleep.

✳ ✳ ✳

Flying down I-10, they make it home in no time. They stop to get gas right before pulling up at home. Marilyn gets out the truck to give David a hug and once again, he stops her and backs up a bit. Marilyn's feelings were hurt and went into the room to lay down. David followed behind her. "Bai, come get in the bed." Marilyn says.

"Nah, I'm good! My stomach hurts and I need to shit!" Marilyn laughs and lays down. "Bai, I need to talk to you!" David called out to Marilyn.

"What's up? What you need to talk about?" Marilyn braces herself.

"My stomach hurts because I've been dreading telling you and don't wanna hurt you. I've been talking to this girl for about a month.

"So, you mean to tell me, you've been talking to somebody and been jumping down my throat like you ain't been doing shit? Who is she and what's her name?" Marilyn goes in.

"Her name is Michelle and I told her everything about you and I from the beginning until now," David responds.

"So, you mean you been telling some bitch you met a month ago all our motherfucking business? Man, nigga you outta there! Y'all fucked?"

"No!"

"You dumb as hell if you think I believe that shit. You got it though!"

Marilyn starts to get her purse so she can get to her nail shop appointment.

"Wait, I wanna talk about this!"

"David, please tell me what else is there to talk about? Here I am being honest about my shit and yo ass been lying the whole time. Go talk to that bitch you've been talking to! Fuck you and her!" Marilyn leaves and makes it to the nail shop. While sitting in the chair, she begins to cry wondering why he would lie this whole time as if he wasn't doing anything. She's done at the nail shop and has arrived back at home. David is sitting in the room still wanting to talk.

"Marilyn, we need to talk!" Marilyn yells loudly, "WHAT THE FUCK DO WE NEED TO TALK ABOUT? I'M DONE TALKING!"

"Okay, well I'm about to go to my dad's house!"

"Does it look like I care? Hell naw. Bye!" Marilyn responds.

She starts to clean up like nothing ever happened. David grabs his backpack and heads to the garage to leave in his car. He kisses all the kids and says, "Daddy loves y'all! I'm going to go see Papaw and I'll see y'all later when I get back." He looks at Marilyn, and she rolls her eyes as he leaves. As it's getting late, although pissed, Marilyn texts David to see if he was on the way home. No response.

Thinking he was being petty by not answering, she texted him again, "Best believe I ain't calling back."

That day would be the last time Marilyn saw David alive.

The night went on and Marilyn eventually fell asleep only to be woken up by the sound of the ambulance and fire trucks flying past their room window. Marilyn didn't think anything of it because they lived right across the street from the police and fire station. As Marilyn tried to go back to sleep, she tossed and turned all night. She felt something was wrong but couldn't put her finger on it. The next morning comes and Marilyn awakes to no David. She begins to text him a total of 12 times and calls him double that. When he didn't return home, she called his father every hour on the hour to see if David was there. Her father-in-law kept reiterating to her that David never showed up at his house. Marilyn thought that was very strange, but her gut knew exactly where he was. With this "Michelle" girl. During the phone call, David's dad blamed her and said, "You know my son loves those kids, if he didn't come home it must've been something you did!" Marilyn hung up on him because she could tell he had been drinking and was not thinking clearly.

Marilyn knew they were going through some rough things at that moment, but ultimately, David was a family man. There was no way he would completely ignore her calls and text messages for too long. The next day went on and still no word from David. Marilyn began to worry as it wasn't like him and another strange feeling took over; therefore, Marilyn called in a missing person report. As the day went on, Marilyn went to clear her mind with her club sisters at a nail shop bar in Pearland, TX. Even in that environment, Marilyn was more focused on the whereabouts of David. Upon arrival back home, Marilyn begins to search through David's email accounts from his laptop, Samsung account, and Metro PCS phone logs hoping to find out who may have been the last person he spoke to. Maybe they had some information on David's whereabouts. She learned that there were 3 people David last spoke to, including Andrea and Becky. Marilyn pondered all day and night searching and trying to figure out where he could be. He wasn't answering his phone and she could see through Gmail's "where's my phone" feature that his phone was dying but it did not show the location of the phone.

Marilyn falls asleep in David's truck waiting on the police to arrive. After waiting for hours, the police showed up at their home a bit after midnight on April 8th. Marilyn wakes up to see bright lights come through the gate. She gets out of the truck to stop them.

"Hello, Officer! Are you looking for 802?" Marilyn asks the officer.

"Yes, are you Mrs. Pickens?" Marilyn nods her head yes.

"Could we step inside your home?"

"Sure!" Marilyn and both officers walk into the apartment and stand in the living room.

"Mrs. Pickens, we need you to verify your name, phone number, David's name, date of birth, and social." Marilyn gives the officer all the information asked. "Did you find David? Is he okay? Where is he?" Marilyn began to ask.

After verifying her information and David's information, they informed Marilyn they had *found* him. *Found? What did they mean, found? Please say he's okay in jail somewhere.* Marilyn thought to herself even though she called the jails and hospitals and he wasn't there.

"I'm sorry to inform you, Mrs. Pickens, but we did find him. David was involved in a head-on car collision early yesterday morning at 1:42am and he did not survive. We have been trying to contact you at a 0948 number." Marilyn was in complete disbelief. So much so that she asked them several times if they were sure it was *her David* involved in this car accident. They assured her it was David and that the car accident wasn't too far from where they lived. The location in which he was and the direction he was driving told Marilyn that David was on his way home. Screaming to the top of her lungs, Marilyn drops to the floor crying.

Marilyn blamed herself. Feeling ten times more guilty than ever before. She thought that if she stopped, took a moment to calm down and listened to him, just maybe he'd be alive. David's sudden death ripped a hole in Marilyn. As more tears began to come, she could not and did not believe this was her reality. Marilyn had mixed feelings about why David passed. One moment she thought God took David away because of his actions. Then she thought God removed David because she truly wasn't supposed to be with him. One thing she was sure of is she had been ignoring the signs to walk away from the relationship all along.

Secrets have a way of revealing themselves. The emails also confirmed his secret affair except it wasn't "Michelle" who he was seeing, it was Becky the assistant. After seeing a post that Becky posted, "Last night was so ratchet, I was forbidden to say anything!" Marilyn put things together but waited until she got her hands on that phone to confirm. There were a lot of emotions running through Marilyn at that time. She experienced one after another. Maybe even simultaneously. She was furious, to say the least. Stuck with all these painful emotions and new information about his affair on top of his sudden death. Marilyn would never have the chance to confront David about his affair or attempt to fully repair the marriage. She started to seek revenge.

The end of the year banquet for Marie's cheer squad was approaching and Marilyn had to reach out to Becky to plan. She had it all figured out. She was going to go up to the podium to hand out awards to the girls with Becky. She then was going to hand one to Becky. "This last award goes to the assistant team mom, Becky here, for not only being a great assistant to me, but an awesome assistant to my husband in bed." And before Becky could realize what was just said, Marilyn was going to drag her ass up and down the gym until she saw blood. However, she didn't want the kids to see that, so she began looking for her address to show up at her doorstep, sit there and upon arrival just start beating her ass. David would be the last husband she'd fuck with when Marilyn got done.

Days after the HPD investigation clearance, Marilyn was able to go to the impound lot where David's Impala was taken to retrieve all of his belongings. When she saw the car, she lost it and although Caleb tried to be strong for his mom, he couldn't hold back the tears either. The car was so smashed and banged up on the front and driver's side, that Marilyn had to squeeze in the driver's side. Anything that allowed Marilyn to feel David's spirit, she did it. Marilyn did not want to leave that car and in that moment, she wanted to go be with David. After being pulled out of the impound lot by Caleb, Ms. Smith, and Munchie, Marilyn's club sister, she finally returned home and got settled.

Marilyn took her time to turn on and unlocked David's phone, it confirmed all her suspicions and brought out the hard truth about him. It also showed that he had been talking to his baby mama while on the way to see Becky. Marilyn found out about all his secrets outside of the affair. She learned all about what he was really doing behind her back. The relationship between him and Andrea was not what she thought. The picture he painted was that they were not able to effectively co-parent. Each of them had a deep disdain for one another. After hearing about David's passing, she came to Marilyn and spilled the truth about the true condition of her and David's relationship. From still being sexually active throughout the years (most recently, being right after Marilyn gave birth to Simone in 2015-16), sleeping in her and her husband's garage without her husband knowing, and lying making it seem like Marilyn was the reason that Angel didn't come around often when it was Marilyn wanting Angel to come over.

Apparently, he confided in Andrea about everything that was going on, including him and his mistress behind Marilyn's back. She knew Andrea wasn't lying because she knew about things that only David could've told her...*including Vernon*. Marilyn was angry, felt betrayed and in that moment, cremation ran through her head so he could burn instead lying peacefully.

CHAPTER 8

THE FUNERAL

After receiving the news of David's death, Marilyn's mother and Pastor Lamont were called to come to the house with Marilyn. After gathering their emotions together, Lamont called the Medical Examiner's Office for information and Marilyn's mother contacted David's mother to give her the news. After that phone call, everybody knew. Marilyn was concerned about how she was going to tell her children about their father's death. Caleb was the one helping Marilyn look for David.

There was never going to be a perfect moment to give her children the heartbreaking news. So, she sucked up her emotions and did what she had to do. Marilyn had her mom, dad, brothers, sister, her friend Crystal, and David's mama were there when the kids got home from school. Marilyn's dad said a prayer and afterwards Marilyn broke the news to the kids.

"So kids, remember how mama was looking for daddy the other day and calling him?"

"Yes ma'am!"

"Do y'all remember where Papa is?"

"Yes ma'am! He's in Heaven now!"

Marilyn began to cry but held it together.

"Your daddy is…" David's mama was about to blurt it out when

Marilyn and Marilyn's mother put their hands up at the same time signaling her to shut up!

"Well, mama found daddy and he is..." Marilyn catches her breath but couldn't control the tears this time. "Mama found him and he's now in heaven with Papa!"

They all started screaming and crying, Caleb fell to his knees as Marilyn's dad tried to catch him. Everybody is now in tears and Marilyn goes outside to get some fresh air. The kids only want her, so they come outside with her as well.

The process of arranging David's funeral was smooth. There were no hiccups outside of his mother wanting to take over the funeral arrangements. She wanted to do things her way rather than being satisfied with just being included. Marilyn wasn't having that. She was his wife and his funeral was going to be exactly the way *he* wanted it to be when he and Marilyn talked about their funerals. During this process, she didn't care for Marilyn's stance towards her. His mom caused all kinds of confusion from the meeting at the funeral home, trying to cause drama between Andrea and Marilyn, not wanting David's dad to be a part of any decisions, etc.

David's mama was just a mean and hateful woman during the planning process. At the wake, she and Marilyn exchanged some pretty rough words. She was upset that David's dad showed up at the funeral home before the public to view his son's body. "I don't know why his ass here! He wasn't invited to be a part of the immediate family to see Jr first." Marilyn heard that and was pissed. She went outside to go get David's dad and walked back in with him to view David. While he was in the viewing room alone with David and David's cousin, Marilyn went back out to address his mama with her mama and Andrea trying to calm her down.

"I told him to come up here to view David first before the rest of the family. David is his got damn son too and YOU of all people know that David didn't play behind his daddy!" said Marilyn.

"I wasn't talking to you wench! You ain't nothing but a wife on paper!" his mama replied.

Marilyn made sure to go in. "Wife on paper? Bitch you ain't nothing but a mama on paper! Bitch, you didn't raise David, he barely had a relationship with your ass. Danielle, David's sister, was his mama. Hell, he didn't even want you around like you think. It was me that talked him into letting you around and being around the kids. Don't act like you forgot how he got in your ass behind picking on my damn daughter. If I were you, I'd keep quiet cause all you've been doing is causing confusion between everybody." Marilyn couldn't believe how ignorant she was acting when she's done nothing but be there for her while being mistreated by her in-laws when her husband passed.

After having to be separated from each other by the funeral director, the wake went according to plan and turned out beautifully. Marilyn did a great job from making sure David looked like himself down to the outfit he had on. The way the car was totaled when Marilyn saw it, God was in that car with David. He had little to no damage to his face and had that same smirk he had when they first met at Walmart ten years prior. That gave Marilyn some peace.

On top of the unnecessary drama his mother was causing, the next day has arrived and the funeral home calls Marilyn to tell her that David's mom had brought them some programs to be passed out at the funeral. However, they did not take them because they weren't the approved programs that Marilyn had one of her church mothers to make. That pissed Marilyn off! "This woman is trying her hardest to piss me off even more!" Crystal calms Marilyn down and once they arrive at the funeral home to start the journey to the church, the funeral director assures Marilyn that those other programs will not be passed out at the church.

Upon arrival at the church, David's mom hops out of the second family car quickly and walks into the church. Andrea comes out to tell Marilyn what's going on. "Marilyn, I don't want you to be upset when you walk in so I'm coming out here to tell you it's being handled. David's mom is in the church passing out her programs to the people. The funeral director is talking to her now and said that if any problems arise that the funeral will be shut down." Marilyn became furious and sent her sister in there to make sure it was handled. Before Marilyn could get out of the car, the funeral director stopped her and told her not to worry and that the other programs would not be read;only the one that she approved. That gave Marilyn some peace, but she wanted that old hag and wanted her *bad.*

It is now time to walk in and Marilyn sees his mom sitting in her spot. Marilyn tells Danielle, "Will you please go tell your mama to move over out of my spot?"

"Marilyn, if I tell her to move over, will you be able to sit there and ignore her?"

"Danielle, I'm good! She just needs to move her ass over!" Danielle goes into the church and makes her mama move over. By now, the tension is thick between all families and everybody is ready to fight...from Marilyn's family who is disgusted by the drama, and David's mama side vs. his daddy side who can't stand each other. As the family walks in, Marilyn's mom gets into it with David's mom on the front row, "Do you mind scooting over so I can sit next to my daughter?"

"If you want to sit next to her, sit behind her cause I ain't moving!"

It took everything in Marilyn's mom not to knock her upside the head. It was to the point where Danielle had to kneel in front of both of them and tell her mom to calm her ass down. She sits in between both. It was just a big mess; however, everyone kept their cool and allowed the service to proceed. Marilyn's uncle is officiating and immediately gets up to pray the tension away. "Now, I have done a lot of funerals, but the tension in here is thick. Now, I know we all loved David, but she (he points to Marilyn) is my niece and he (pointing to David) is my nephew. My niece has entrusted me to run this funeral and because I knew how David was, we're going according to what this program says (he holds the program up that Marilyn approved) and send my nephew on to glory. Now before we start, this may be out of order and I'm still going to go according to the program, but I'm going to pray this uneasy spirit away." The audience claps in agreement and after he prays, the funeral continues.

* * *

The funeral is now over, and they head to the burial site. Because his mom passed out her programs that had the wrong location on it, more confusion arises, and some people made it at the end or missed the burial. David is now laid to rest and all the families go their separate ways. Marilyn's family and friends went to the repass at her church, and David's dad side had their own get-together, which Marilyn and the kids would come to later that night. David's mom's side did whatever they did. It's crazy but in all this drama, the one person that has helped Marilyn deal with it all is Andrea. Since David's death, she's been helpful. Marilyn and Andrea decided to keep in contact for the sake of their children. The best thing in all of this was Angel wanting to be around Marilyn and the kids all the time. That was the best feeling Marilyn could ever feel as she was not going to forget about Angel. She still looked at her as the 3-year-old that she first met ten years ago.

CHAPTER 9
TRUST THE PROCESS

When Marilyn finally had a chance to sit in all this and sort through her feelings, facing the truth was hard. She could not be mad that David was confiding in Andrea because she was confiding in Vernon. They both were cheating on one another emotionally. She should have been honest with David from the beginning and he should have done the same. There they were building a life and a family together and were both giving their hearts and emotional energy to another person throughout their relationship, before and after marriage. He would go the extra mile several times and cheat physically. It was pointless to be together. At the time, Marilyn did not think that what she was doing was considered cheating by staying in contact with Vernon. Although Marilyn and David kept attempting to make things work at different stages of their relationship, it was never on the same page at the same time. No matter how much she tried to excuse herself from the wrongdoing, the facts proved that she was just as wrong as David. Their whole 10-year relationship never had a fair chance to survive.

After the funeral, Marilyn didn't want to talk to anyone. All she was concerned about was stabilizing herself and her children. News reporters would soon start to reach out and after the first two interviews, Marilyn was tired of talking about David's death. The pain was unbearable. She thought about Vernon, but felt too guilty to try to be in a relationship with him and really didn't want to deal with him at all. Marilyn felt it would be a slap in the face to David. Her vulnerability led her further into the arms of TGG. TGG was tall, sweet, and very charismatic – a cool and kind-hearted individual. He and Marilyn would talk all the time, more so away from the set because folks would be all in the mix. Things would become sexual with the two of them and with each encounter, whether through general conversation or intimacy, he would be the reason Marilyn began to smile again. In Marilyn's mind, things between the two of them were great and low-key. However, Vernon was pulling at her heart all while the pain of David's death was ripping her apart. She was so confused about what to do that she began reaching out to a medium, looking for guidance and answers. Grief will make you do things you would not normally consider, but she would be the reason that Marilyn is still able to talk to David through reading sessions.

✳ ✳ ✳

Two weeks after David's funeral, Marilyn got a phone call from an irritated Vernon. Thinking he was calling in response to her 911 "Vernon" JPay, he called to tell her that he did not want to deal with her anymore because he felt she was giving him the runaround.

"Hello!" says Marilyn as she answers the phone.

"Hey! What's up my baby? Look man, I'ma get to the point because it's hurting me to even tell you this." Vernon tells Marilyn. Marilyn is thrown off because she's never heard him talk like this, especially to her. "We've been at this back and forth for 13 years now. I'm tired of my heart being taken for granted and I can't do the run around anymore." Marilyn cuts Vernon off. "Vernon, what are you talking about? I'm not taking your heart for granted."

Although she knew what he was saying, it's not something she wanted to hear at the moment. "Marilyn, I think we should focus on being friends until you fully decide what you want to do concerning us." In all fairness, Marilyn could not be upset with him. All the back and forth between the two of them, not giving a second thought to the damage she was doing to herself and both men. In the same conversation, she told Vernon that David had passed. He didn't believe her at first.

"Vernon, I cherish your feelings and I understand but I need to talk to you. David was involved in a head on collision and didn't make it." Both get quiet.

"Marilyn, stop playing! That's not funny. Why would you say some shit like that?" Vernon responds.

"Vernon, I have no reason to make that up. Why would I make up some shit about my kids' father being killed? I don't know what to do. I blame myself! HE'S GONE AND I DO NOT WANT TO BE HERE ANYMORE!" Marilyn yells out.

When he noticed her tone went up and the story hadn't changed, he was more compassionate towards her loss. "My God! Baby, I'm sorry! I hate that this happened. Where are you? Where are the kids? Are they okay? If you're driving, I need you to pull over and calm down. Think about the kids! They need you more now. Their dad is gone and you can't go with him. Who gon take care of the kids the way you and David did? You are stronger than this baby! Forget about me, it's about you and those kids now. If you didn't pull over, go home until the kids get home."

Marilyn didn't say a word. She just followed his instructions and went home until the kids got out of school. "Marilyn, I love you and pray you begin to be okay for the kids. I'll be right here for you."

Vernon seemed to be genuinely concerned about how Marilyn was managing day by day. From that moment on, he would call and check on her everyday. For the majority of her days, Marilyn would cry her eyes out. For two months straight she would drive Hwy 249 at the same time and speed she believed David to be driving, in the same lane David was in just to be in that moment with him. Several times, she thought about killing herself. She would shut herself off from everyone and only wanted to be around her kids. No one else mattered. Not even Vernon and she would begin to ignore his calls. Marilyn also left the social club she was in. That was another weight lifted off her as she knew David couldn't stand the set.

CHAPTER 10
INFINITY LOVE

Finally, in August 2019, Marilyn decided to follow her heart. She stopped holding back about how she really felt about Vernon. She'd been battling with herself about sharing her truth with anyone for a very long time. She feared the judgment she'd get based on the circumstances Vernon was in. That was an exhausting effort. She sat down and wrote him a long letter through JPay.

Vernon! I know I've been distant. I can't sleep and because you're on my mind heavy, I decided I wanted to reiterate just how much I love you. No matter how much I tried to deny you or even walk away from you, I found myself right back to you. The intimacy you provide me without getting sexual is everything to me. You are a part of me as I am to you! I love you so much! Babe, the truth, as you already know, is that I'm afraid to receive your love and to give you my love, wholeheartedly. David's tragedy has fucked me up and I'm afraid to lose you. The relationship you and I have has never wavered in a sense but still, I'm afraid.

As you said last night, we now have absolutely nothing standing in our way, yet I'm afraid. I love you unconditionally and I'm also afraid that the next level our love takes us will be so breathtaking that I can't deal with it. In a sense, I'm running but at a standstill. Jogging in place. Will I hurt you, again? No. Do I believe you will hurt me? No. You called and asked me "Will I marry you?" I told you to stop playing with me and said yes. Do I see you as my husband? Yes. Do I see our future? Yes. Do I love everything about you, whether good or bad? Yes. Do I trust you? Yes. I'm just afraid. Afraid to take a real risk, afraid to be open and vulnerable to you by allowing your love in all the way, and afraid to lose you.

The things you say to me are exactly what I need to hear and love to hear. India Arie's "Truth" is all you and THAT scares me. As a young girl growing up, I will say that I feel I didn't get the "love" I needed from my parents. Growing up, I yearned for real love and wanted someone to love me unconditionally, in which having Caleb made me feel that I would finally get that. He would never turn his back on me and love me for me. Back then, I figured the love my son has for me was enough. Then, I began to realize there was a different kind of love that a child can't give you and that's when I begin to be in search of something that was never sincere or real.

Then you came along, gave me that in a short time, which was taken away, then I was back searching again. Got with David and you know what that has been like (good and bad). During those years with him, you've always managed to still give me what I needed. Sometimes, I obliged; other times, I was confused because of the situation. Now we're here. Again, nothing or no one in the way, yet I'm STILL afraid. Years ago, we would tell each other not to "turn the page" or in my case "only flipping the corners down". I think now, it's time we close the entire book and start a new book; however, I do feel I'm more than a handful and although you say you can handle it, I'm afraid it may push you away. My antics aren't average. I'm not average. I love you so much, Vernon! I really do, unconditionally! I'm ready to give it all to you, I'm just afraid of the realness behind it all.

Marilyn would soon get a response to the letter she wrote him. Checking the mailbox, the letter reads:

Marilyn, when I tell you I love you I want it to mean more than anyone else in the whole world who says it. I want it to mean that your happiness is everything to me and that I only want the best for you and the kids always no matter what it takes. I want it to mean that you are more important to me than anything else in my life. When I tell you I love you, I want it to mean that you are a part of me, and I am a part of you. No matter what happens in this world we'll always be together forever sharing our lives and our happiness.

Baby girl, you really have me open literally I feel like I have finally found my way back into your realm. I really enjoyed everything we talked about and shared. I always want us to share each other's world, thoughts and feelings. I promise you won't lose me. Ever! Right now, I'm just smiling hard, cheesed up thinking of you. The sound of your voice, my favorite song only you know how to sing, I want you to sing for me every day if you will so kindly. Marilyn, you are my world! Feelings are just so all over me for you right now. I love you so much and there's nothing you can do about it. Applauding you with my heartbeat for never forgetting about me!

That alone shows me how much I mean to your world. The best and most beautiful things in the world cannot be seen or even touched. They must be felt with the heart! You are the best; you are the most beautiful. Every time I think of those things like now, my heart just gets excited!! You Marilyn, you are a beautiful woman inside and out. I feel that I have to sprint just to keep up with your jogging. You affect me profoundly. You have loved me through a thousand trials and you deserve all that I must give. You are always on time and I can't wait no more until we both make good on the promises we gave each other. What we share is so rare but it's our truth. Every love story is beautiful, but ours is my favorite. You know you found true love when you catch yourself falling in love with the same person over and over again.

It's clear that neither of us can control what is happening between us again and again. I love you and miss you so and I can't wait until it's official Mrs.Marilyn Ray once and for all. Our happiness grows every day even through the minor disagreements which you always win. I love you! I'm about to go to sleep with a smile on my face.
Two hearts = one love
Missing you crazy always mine, forever yours
Vernon, Your Truth

✳ ✳ ✳

Over the next few weeks, Marilyn and Vernon go through the necessary steps to finally become husband and wife. Something they have wanted since the beginning, thirteen years ago. The day has come for Vernon and Marilyn to become one. Marilyn and her friend, Shuntell, arrive at the unit. After going through security, Marilyn along with the minister, and a Sergeant sit in the visitation area waiting for Vernon to come through the doors. Marilyn is nervous but excited to hug Vernon again after 13 years.

He walks through the door smiling hard as hell, but Marilyn can tell he's nervous. He takes his time approaching her. Marilyn gets up from the table and runs to him, jumping in his arms. Even though she wasn't supposed to do that, the Sergeant started laughing and didn't mind. She gave him the biggest kiss, but had to refrain herself. They then begin the ceremony. Vernon read his vows,

I don't ever want to take you for granted. I don't ever want to forget what it was like before you or how it would be without you. I don't ever want to forget our first kiss or our last touch, or let a day go by without telling you how much you mean to me, how deeply I love you and how much I need you. I don't ever want you to doubt the way I feel or how much happier I am because of you. When I tell you I love you, I want it to mean more than when anyone else in the whole world says it. I want it to mean that your happiness is everything to me and that I only want the best for you always, no matter what it takes.

I want it to mean that you're more important to me than anything else in my life after God. When I tell you I love you, I want it to mean that you are a part of me and I am a part of you. And no matter what happens in this world, we'll be together forever sharing our lives and our happiness. I love you, Butterfly. You deserve every beat of my heart. I love you because I want to help you reach your goals and protect you from your fears. I promise to always treat you with respect, love every part of you, and to always live by loyalty, honesty, and trust when it comes to our marriage.

I accept you for the person you are and I don't wish to change you into someone else. I promise to love you and stand by your side even when I'm working on your nerves and are too tired to do the things I need you to do. This is just a small note of what you mean to me today and always. I love you baby!

Marilyn read hers:

What does it take to have a good marriage? A good marriage begins with two good people. It takes trust, laughter, and compromise. It's finding friendship and romance in the same person's smile. It's loving unconditionally. It's remembering what matters and forgetting what doesn't. It's filling life with what you love and loving who you're with. A good marriage begins with two good people like you and I. Baby, I love you so much! Thank you for finding me in 2006 and claiming me as your good thing from the moment you saw me. Thank you for standing feet planted through all these years through my good and through my bad. Thank you for pouring into me and for allowing me to pour into you. Provide. Offer. Uplift and Rebuild. You're the best, you're my lifeline, you're my all. I love you Mr. Ray!

Both were waiting on one thing, to kiss the hell out of each other. Standing there looking into each other's eyes, Vernon drops a few tears. Marilyn wipes them away and mouths, "I love you so much!" Vernon says back, "I love you too!"

"You may now kiss your ...." The minister couldn't get her words out quick enough before Marilyn and Vernon were locking lips. This was an exceedingly long time coming. They kept going like no one was in the room but them until the sergeant finally said something. They would get 30 minutes to sit and talk. All they did was hold hands, never wanting to let go, looking in each other's eyes and both begin to shed tears. They were happy and living in that moment. A moment lasting forever. They are now ready to start their life as Mr. & Mrs. Vernon Ray. Marilyn makes it back home and has a letter waiting for her:

Baby Girl, by the time you get this, you will be officially Mrs. Ray!

You are finally all mine!! "WOW" I knew when I first met you, I knew that I would fall in love with you and make you mine. For a second, I doubted that you would fall in love with me. But once we finally gelled, it was clear that neither of us could control what was happening to us. What was true love showed up and showed out. True love is action. True love is loyalty. MY TRUE LOVE was being patient because I knew in my HEART that you were always mine, only mine, and all mine. You used to joke about me putting voodoo on you, but I don't practice that. This is genuine, real love. We're married now and that is one of the greatest joys in my life besides seeing my son being born. Baby girl, I value you and our marriage. Thank you so much for loving me and for believing in me. Thank you for allowing me to hold you and the kids in my heart. I love you all so much!

Love conquers all! ALWAYS MINE, FOREVER YOURS.
Your HUSBAND, Vernon, Your Truth

Marilyn wastes no time writing him back.

~ Happiness ~
Baabyyy!! I love you. Today was perfect! Thank you for being soft with me. Genuine with me. Loving me. The way you talk about

me to others in front of me and when I'm not around fills my heart with more butterflies. But most importantly, thank you for making me YOUR wife. Thank you, baby. I couldn't stop smiling thinking about you on the way home. Was a bit worried because you didn't call but figured they racked y'all up because of the shortage of staff. Nevertheless, I smiled the entire way home and am still smiling. I'm on cloud 1,000. I love me some you. The way you kiss me so passionately and soft helps me feel our soul connecting. I love you so much baby and I thank you for waiting on your Queen. You have the world at your feet baby and I promise to make sure you're treated like the King God created for me. I thank God so much for you. I love you.

Your Wife,
The REAL & ONLY Mrs. Marilyn Ray

REMOVING THE VEIL

In life, we are given options. Options that include following your heart or your mind. Marilyn knew in her heart that Vernon was the one and was willing to go through his sentence with him, yet she followed her mind and chose the option to rock with David for ten years knowing they should've remained friends. Loving someone and lusting over someone are two different things, but have the same powerful outcome. If not careful with the two, you'll end up lying to yourself and hurting those involved.

Marilyn feels free beyond the word itself; however, she has some more healing to do. The grateful thing is, she now has the love of her life helping her get through the loss, hurt, and pain of David with prayer, words of encouragement, and being a listening ear. Her beloved gives her space when she needs it, allowing her to scream her emotions out when life becomes overwhelming.

Masking is never a good idea as it also leads to self turmoil. Don't be like Marilyn and allow a veil to be placed over your face only to be removed ten years later. If you must, pray and ask God for signs. In the words of Brigitte Nicole, if you don't follow your heart, you might spend the rest of your life wishing you had.

ABOUT THE AUTHOR

Born in Houston, Texas, Niesha M. Taylor is the second oldest of five and stands on the shoulders of the strong women before her, her mom and grandmothers. As the wife to Gregory V. Ray, Sr., super mom to Khallid, Daijah, A'niya, King David, Laiya, bonus daughter Alicia, best selling author, and founder/president/ceo of a non-profit, Angel of Mine Foundation, Niesha is determined to follow her passion in life by helping others discover who they are by encouraging them to go after what they want in life, whether it's true love or their dreams. Not realizing it would be her own story, Niesha hopes that by telling her unapologetic truth that it touches at least one person and transforms their way of thinking.

She came. She saw. She's conquering.